COLORS OF
THE SOUL

COLORS OF
THE SOUL

by
R. J. MATTHEWS

COLORS OF THE SOUL

ISBN: 978-0-9980965-3-7

Copy editing by Taynia L. Shoebotham

Cover design by Taynia L. Shoebotham

COLORS OF
THE SOUL

CLEAR AS GRAY

Here we go.

I am still me, well sorta. I was born like everyone else. I think I was born or it is a really good implanted memory. A memory along with the millions of other memories that I can recall anytime throughout the day. Well, ok, I don't exactly remember my birth even though I know I was there. But who really can remember that far back? Come on, I would be lying to you if I said I did. I think I'm still human but at some point, I received some nifty enhancements. But I will get to that later.

And yes, in case you were wondering, I am not alone. There are many of us like me in some shape or fashion, in everyday life and in every corner of the world. There may be one at your workplace or the person you passed on the highway on your morning commute. It is not like we each carry a big sign that says, "I am an Immortal." As for myself, I personally would sport a t-shirt that would say something like that on the front. Just to be a funny guy. That was a joke, why aren't you laughing?

Can we at least agree I think I was human at some point in my life? I never really ponder about the concept of life much anymore as my top deep-thinking priorities have shifted ever so slightly. Well, a lot. I don't think about time much either and I certainly don't own a watch. Who really wears a watch in this day and age anyways? Use your cell phone if you want to know the time.

1

You see, I can be considered immortal, you know the type: can't die, live forever, etc. You may want to write this down. Important point, remember it and don't forget it: I am not God nor am I a god. The big guy is still up there in heaven and, whatever religious following you donate to on the weekends, he still exists in all his glorious aspects. I have to tell the atheists all the time, "you've got it all wrong." I also know God is listening to me right now and I don't want him to take away my immortality card.

Oh yes, getting back to the immortality part. Here is the kicker, the cosmic joke. It works great...until it doesn't. At least I think I am still immortal; I have proven it many, many times before so it is still working for me. Cross my fingers. It is still something I don't take lightly and test out every so often just for the hell of it. It is not like I come from a race of Immortals. It simply became the rule of law when I woke up one day. Yep, as simple as that. Like sleeping. You simply do it and not think about it anymore (except for in dreams as I guess you do think while sleeping).

Of course, one could also argue the whole idea of which is the true reality and which is dreamland but that's not the point I am trying to make. We can debate about that one later as I have nothing booked in my appointment calendar next week. Do you? I do hope you are writing all of this down or making a list on what to discuss at a future time. I have all the free time in the world, how about you?

There are rules to being one of the Immortals. No, I did not get a handbook in the mail nor did I have to take a class at the local community college. These rules simply exist for a reason and to set some boundaries. Some of them I was told by others and some of them, sadly, I had to figure out the hard way. For example, I can transcend good old planet Earth. But outer space is boring and empty so I stopped visiting it ages ago. Plus, it's really cold too. Along with outer space, anything with extremes like the bottom of the ocean, the artic, a volcano, or space I tend to start losing consciousness and fade away so I no longer attempt to explore any of those places. Why should I when I can be extremely happy visiting the millions of happy and cool, even fun parts of this world? The South Pacific islands come to mind. You catch what I am saying? Fun, cool places and it's free for me. What a deal!

With that being said, traveling the immortal way can be quite tricky and it takes hundreds of years to skillfully master it. Most of us don't have that much time to work on our long-distance traveling skills as we often 'recycled' or taken out before such long periods of time. By taken out I mean killed. Die. Terminated. Immortal card revoked.

However, I will give you the basics on my immortal travel but it can be different for others. I once saw a dude flap his arms and fly like a bird, but I digress. I can currently move short distances…well what I call short distances. I can and do pop into New York City on occasion to catch a Broadway play every now and then. However, in traversing an entire continent at once, well, that would take considerable energy and it would wear me down for days. I find it much easier to book a plane ticket especially if going overseas. Plus, I get frequent flyer miles. The other flyer miles!

Here is a quick history lesson for the day: there have always been Immortals among us roaming around throughout history. You may have read about them in books and stories passed along throughout the ages. You may have even witnessed some in real life. My brethren and I have been blending in among the rest of the population since the beginning of time. Believe it if you want to or not. It is a simple fact of life and I have certainty lived a longer life than you have. We go by such familiar names you may recognize: angels, saints, ghosts, vampires, and werewolves. Those are the easy ones. You'll probably find it surprising that on the same list are some overly paid actors and actresses who can't act at all, some really talented people at sports (no names!) and a few select musicians (the majority actually have talent). One often wonders how these celebrities were so popular when no one has ever claimed to buy their albums or watch their movies. You often hear that a particular celebrity must have made a deal with the devil. I tell you that if I were the Devil, I would never sign half of the sports folks to any sort of contract. So, is it starting to make sense to you? Shall we press on because there is so much more.

The personnel list is endless and these folks were always found to be my brethren, and most of them prefer to keep the secret to ourselves. We only dabble in the spotlight or in human drama every once in a while, usually when we are bored or when there are some really bad people doing really dreadful things to another human. Immortality is quite boring most of the time hence why someone 'higher up' thought it would be better to put us to good use. This is the part about dabbling in other human lives. We don't question it when we have to "take an assignment" and it is not for us to judge. We are only there to act upon the grave act that is transpiring in front of us. It's our job, after all.

As you can see, after flying around and seeing every major world landmark, scaring the 'Bee-Jesus' out of common folks, stealing money from banks or the criminal element to accumulate wealth, I feel there is something more important we Immortals must do. We establish our individual kingdoms and places to store our "worldly possessions" and we often chart out incredible and reclusive retreats on remote islands or other exotic locales on this planet. That's what it really boils down to in the grand scheme of things. I have a great island retreat with open air windows. You really should visit it sometime. I have other places to live in around the USA and around parts of the world but you are not allowed the keys to those. Well, not yet unless you want a short-term lease. I promise I will offer you a good deal. Trust me, why would I cheat you?

Of course, there is playing and running around with the other Immortals but that grows tiresome too. Pistol duels are boring until someone's immortality sudden expires…then the duel becomes a lot more interesting. Many of us do not form long or intimate friendships or bonds with other Immortals. It takes the fun out of it when someone is just as powerful as yourself. Everyone wants to drive recklessly. Why not, we ain't gonna die?

We really prefer to keep to ourselves and, more often than not, have normal, human companions. I have come across a few of my kind in my time and chatted with them for a bit, tipped my hat and continued on. I think I watched a Monday Night Football game with another at a bar once as it was mind-numbing on a Monday night with nothing to do. I guess he did not feel like flying around the world or scaring mortals either. We do normal things…sometimes. I guess it keeps us from disagreeing amongst ourselves which would the lead to alliances forming and then eventually to war between us. Can you imagine what the world would look like with a bunch of Immortals fighting it out? Not pretty at all, to say the least!

Like I said earlier, time is not important to us Immortals anymore. We prefer to think on an event timeline. Not hour-to-hour or day-to-day. After all, we've got all the time in the world to do anything. Some of my kind have figured out how to go back and forward through time. Now that's a scary thought!

Now this leads to the purpose. There is always that catch, isn't there? Are you still there? Do you want me to continue on? Thought so. Ok, here is the purpose. Oh wait; let us take a five-minute break. Have a snack and a drink and we can resume in a few minutes.

I hope you are refreshed and sated. Now sit back, relax, and listen to the explanation on the purpose. Here is the golden answer: we have no idea why. One can question everything in the world and why things happen. We have been discussing this for ages and it is the main topic of discussion every time when we see one of our own kind. Except nobody has figured out a master plan or ultimate answer. It is simply the way it is. Once we figure it out, I swear it will be aired as "Breaking News."

Now some of us may have exploited their "gift" for monetary value and accumulated millions or even billions of dollars. Have you ever wondered about some of those rich people and celebrities that have accumulated all this wealth yet die "mysteriously" i.e. accidental death, random shooting and so on? Do you now think it was really accidental or not?

I could go on and list some of the names but this is not a monologue into the Who's Who of the Immortals. If you do become one, some of this will be revealed to you. And you will probably be right on a lot of guesses: yes to the one computer geek worth a lot of money, yes to the one musician with the cheesy hit

6

song and, oh yes, that other female you are thinking about, yep, you don't even have to ask. Now it all is starting to make sense, right?

Let us review what else you know about us other than we call ourselves Immortals. Well, actually, we call ourselves Bob, Fred, Julie etc. Note: if you ever meet any of those three I just mentioned, pretend you do not know that they are immortal and you certainly did not hear from me, much appreciated.

I bet you are still thinking about what I said earlier about how we travel. Well, we can walk, ride a bike, drive a car, or even fly in a plane. We can also move at near hypersonic speed and appear half way around the country over a short period of time. It does wreak havoc with modern radar systems however, so we try to keep the speeds down. As for myself, I've probably been logged numerous times in some CQ logbook as an 'unexplained' phenomena.

Of course, it is rather like riding a bike. There is a learning process that takes years to master. I once overshot Chicago enroute from Kansas City and ended up landing in the metro-Detroit area. Yes, yes, good thing I am immortal as that is the only way to survive in Detroit…but there is the really incredible Greek section in downtown Detroit you must add to your bucket list. I'm telling you, you definitely have to visit. I think it is aptly called Greektown. But I digress – you know, marinated lamb is quite the distraction. I am better at my landings now and can usually get within 500 feet…give or take a 2-mile radius. What? You think that's bad? Well, trying doing it in the rain or through a thunderstorm. Go ahead, I challenge you.

The traveling and appearing instantaneously in new areas is rather fun, and, it never gets old. It is like you think of the location and, suddenly, you are there. There is no other way to describe it. Sadly, I do not appear in a plume of smoke or riding along a lightning bolt but I really need to learn to do both someday. I also do have not a welcoming committee with cheerleaders or a band playing a college fight song when I materialize. I merely appear and blend in. That is pretty much it on the speed "we" can travel or should I say specifically, how "I" travel. I don't know, maybe all of us or none of us can travel like I do. That would be a travesty, well, for them. It is much too fast for the human eye and I generate zero carbon emissions.

Oh sure, I've probably startled a few people here and there. They might have even taken a photo, but, all you would see is a blurry image. They either forget about it or keep it to themselves or join the local conspiracy theory support group. Which is a good thing. I would feel bad if I started a panic after telling them I am the guy in the blurry image jetting across the sky.

The traveling is fun and quite efficient. Think about my carbon footprint versus yours. See? I am doing my part to save the planet. I should get a medal or something. However, I don't go buzzing around anymore like the olden days. It fatigues me and expends vast amounts of my energy needlessly. I do it now only for need or to impress a girl here and there. A guy will do anything to secure that second date. What is your nifty trick?

In my early years way back when I got the gift, I once tried to traverse Mt Everest. Of course, it wasn't called Mt Everest back then. However, in the end, this was a bad idea. Thanks to the chilly air and the lack of oxygen for which I was not prepared, my mind and body started shutting down. So much for immortality. I guess in the grand design, the physical nature of us Immortals cannot overcome the basic rules of nature. The next time I did it many years later, I brought along a jacket that was bought legitimately from REI and an oxygen mask that was stolen. The view is so amazing up there; you will have to get up there some time. Trust me, you will love it!

You are probably thinking right now that I have contradicted myself. How can the forces of nature harm me – i.e. the extreme conditions on Mt Everest – when I am supposed to be immortal? I don't have a great answer for that; I am Immortal not Einstein. However, I will say in the end, nature always wins. I stopped going into outer space (remember, I said it was boring) and I stopped going to places where humans weren't designed to go unprotected in the first place. Do I really want my immortality to stop when I am 10,000 feet below sea level? Hell no! Neither would you! Stop asking questions about where to travel and plainly accept I can go where most humans can. Point closed.

What's that you say? You want me to clarify the immortality thing again? Well, we live our life as Immortals until we die. Kinda funny, isn't it? I have lived for a long time and stopped celebrating my birthday decades ago. We are supposed to be immortal and not die but we can and will die eventually. That's a depressing thought. Let's move on to more cheerful thoughts. To some, it can be over 1,000 years and, to others, it is a really short period of time. I've heard many times over this rumor about a guy named Dwayne who was said to have the shortest period of immortality. How short was it? Exactly one month, literally 30 days.

When some discover the immortal gift, they go down to the rough part of towns and get shot up, run in front of cars purposely not dodging traffic or other such crazy, daredevil activities. But not

Dwayne. His immortality was apparently not 100% charged and he tried to fly across a railroad track on a dirt bike using a ramp he specifically built while, if you can believe it, filming it. The footage is pretty cool, search for it on YouTube, right up until Dwayne gets nailed by the fast-moving train. It is now a running joke to ask how many Dwayne Days they have to go before they are considered in the "safe" zone. I always tip my hat to honor Dwayne when I see a fast-moving train. Some people just never have any luck, do they?

On the other end of the spectrum, there are people out there claiming to be over 1,000 years old. Like I said before, time ceases to be of any importance to us after a while. We could sleep for months or years and wake up, mess about, and go right back to sleep for a year or two. It is not like we need sleep but it is a valuable time for us to rest our minds and silence all the noise for a bit. This leads us to one of the most unique talents of the Immortals. This gift is one we have learned to quickly adapt to before it drives us insane.

Imagine being on the beach in a secluded part of the world. You are the only one on this beach and the island for that matter. It is a beautiful day with few clouds in the sky; the sun is beating down on your skin warming you to a comfortable temperature. The waves gently crash in the background calming you with their sound. It is truly paradise. Now imagine you are at a Metallica concert and the band is playing "Master of Puppets" CHA CHA CHA…the guitar riffs are gutting the sound system and the songs are echoing throughout the venue as the entire crowd is belting out the words in a cacophony of intense and ear-piercing noise.

Now that I made the comparison of two opposite sides of the spectrum, I want to give the differences of when our "special talent" is truly on as opposed to what it is like when it is off. So, what happens when the talent turns on? Something amazing, that's what. I like to think of it as our real purpose and being. No, it is not to annoy or haunt humans. Rather this talent seeks out the raw, negative energy transferred from human to human. In layman's terms, it is the evil and violence that one human is inflicting on the other that becomes a beacon for my kind to be drawn there. The intensity sometimes is unfathomable and we are literally pulled to the spot. However, the degree to which it moves us and whom it decides to move is one of the greatest mysteries. Some wise guys suggested it was like requesting an Uber vehicle and one of any number of vehicles pings the request first. I wouldn't know as I have no need for Uber. We have no settings to adjust it but it makes it easier when only one of us is driven to the source versus all of us from around the world being driven to one spot. I guess someone did think of everything. Maybe it was the same technology as Uber. Wait a minute, is one of the original programmers for Uber an Immortal?

This gift is a curse and a blessing.

When I switch it on, the noise is indescribable. It is best defined as hearing the roaring din of sounds at a rock concert. OMG, it is so intense it actually causes me pain and suffering. It is nothing like anything you could possibly imagine or dream of. Yes, it is that bad and yes, I have to respond to it. The source of evil and malicious intent against a fellow man, or woman in so many cases, literally is a force I can't deny.

Luckily, this can be turned off so I don't have to listen to it 24-7. The downside is the guilt that accompanies it. It stems from the fact I willingly did nothing when I knew something was going down and a person most likely was harmed to some degree. It happens all the time and I try not to get too emotional about it. I may not have prevented what was fated to be, fated to happen. Of course, we can't have it off forever because we start to get punishments for having it off. An awful itch, constant sneezing, hiccups, pains, etc. See, the universe has balance after all. If we Immortals are supposed to have the talent turned on to responds to cries then rightly so we are punished for turning it off for a prolonged period of time.

Hey, I am only here to clean up the really, really messed-up cases or the ones that have some profound influence later in life. You have no idea how many of those type of cases I have had to deal with, especially within the past year. If you think the world is messed up, try to imagine how many of those that I didn't have time to remedy, fix, or alleviate. More importantly, sometimes the desire to be truly human supersedes anything. We are great actors and we can play the human part so well, often for such prolonged periods of time, that sometimes, we actually begin to believe we are normal humans. In the end, our true nature comes out and we have to make a choice. But, isn't life all about making choices?

Let me recount an incident that happened a while back. I turned on my talent one night and it was like listening to the police scanner. All of a sudden, there were six different domestic disputes, umpteen arguments between couples at a local eatery and a handful of fights in various stages between couples, friends, mates, roommates, and casual strangers. In other words, a normal night when the talent is turned on. So, where should I begin? Which fires should I put out? I was ready to swarm in and start scanning the scenarios when one unique case crossed my "airwaves."

This happened some time ago. Remember what I said earlier, time is meaningless to me so I cannot recall the exact day or even the year when it happened. What I can tell you is that her name was Tonya and she was moments away from achieving her ultimate and final accomplishment, suicide. It was time to intervene and stop her from finishing the deed but, then again, maybe it was already too late to help her. I still had to try I suppose.

A little background story on Tonya is in order.

Tonya had it all as far as most females go. She was smart yet sassy. She was beautiful but did not let it go to her head too much. And, of course, she fell for the wrong man early in life and worked a dead-end job.

He wasn't just the wrong man, rather, he was a Class A dipshit. But, he promoted the tough guy persona and she ate it up like it was a cheap Chinese buffet. When people are in love or in the idea of love, they are clouded by their judgement and often go ignoring all the classic signs of an unhealthy relationship.

Well, sorry Tonya. Most of your friends would have told you to dump this sorry ass of a man. In fact, your best friend, Susie, even told you last week to "be careful." But you never heed anyone's advice. You always thought you knew best and could make the decisions all by yourself.

What does it matter what those other people think? They don't know him like I know him? He is……. blah……. blah….and more blah.

13

Ok, I have been around for quite a while and heard this from more than one female in my considerable lifetime. It is no secret surprise or grand epiphany. Well, Tonya was spouting out these words after ignoring the pleas from her best mates warning.

Well, Tonya. Can't say they didn't warn you. You never listened to their advice, did you? Now look where that has got you?

Fast forward to the current predicament.

I feel the suffering from Tonya and pick up on the vibrations almost immediately. I think I am meant to be the one to intercept her cry for help, her plea in her last, few, precious moments of life.

It takes only a matter of minutes from the initial plea, to me receiving it, all the way to my reaction and movement towards her small apartment on the south side of town.

I land with my feet on the ground in the hallway a few feet away from her door and walk the few paces until I stand in front of her apartment. I hesitate to knock because it seems rude to do so, but, I feel the pain of her plight and enter the apartment unannounced. Note: I am not a vampire and do not have to worry about being invited to enter a dwelling. I am sure there are books and television shows if you are into that sorta thing. I can enter any dwelling of my choosing just like, oh, any other normal person can and does. Unless, of course, it's not their house. I do not own her apartment and entering it for me, at this moment, is still very illegal. The law is the law and don't assume the law I follow is from the movies or Internet.

Despite the law, I proceed to enter her apartment unannounced. I move past the modest living room and small kitchen as she is not in either. Easy enough, genius, that leaves only the bedroom or the bathroom. I'd rather not catch her in the act of her indiscretion. I only hope she is in the bedroom having a bad dream or something benign. However, for me to pick up such strong vibrations on the immortal network, would suggest that she is both conscience and alive at least for the moment. Which means I should go check the bathroom.

Oh dear, the worse place to surprise someone, especially someone like myself. No need to knock as that would scare her even more. Talk about creepy. One knows they live alone and is in the bathroom doing bathroom stuff. To hear a sudden knock on the bathroom door, would give anyone a heart attack right there on the spot.

Having passed the bedroom with no sign of Tonya, I decide to enter the bathroom in hopes of saving a life and hopefully not causing her any embarrassment.

I instantly appear beyond the bathroom door as I'm too lazy to open it. Lucky for me it was a spacious bathroom. At least she is not sitting down.

Tonya screams in terror as she is about to slice her precious wrist wide open with the razor blade held tightly in her other hand.

I can't think of anything cool or sly to say so I give the most nonchalant response ever posed by man. Just note it doesn't work in bars on the ladies either.

"Hey, how's it going?" I am so glad I am not trying to pick up Tonya in a bar or at a nightclub.

Tonya is still screaming at the top of her lungs but oddly the sound is not all that loud. That's strange. Her nearly white eyes are fixated on me. Her hand holds the blade firmly but her brain has switched modes and is now thinking about using the blade in a defensive posture. Which really is surprising given the fact she was mere seconds away from offing herself with that very same blade.

"Tonya." I immediately say as if it will calm her down. Sadly, it does not. She is breathing rapidly and shock is starting to set in.

Ok. I try a different tact on her.

"Tonya. I am not going to hurt you and I want to help you." There, that should do the trick. Who wouldn't be comforted by that type of patronizing reply.

Tonya freezes right away. Most likely it is not from the fact that she believes anything at the moment. Or even registering anything I am saying but is more confused as to why I keep speaking her name, her proper name.

Well, I score points in that I stopped her from slicing her wrists and I have her attention for a split second. It's as if she is waiting for me to make the next move. I better play this smoothly and quickly.

"Tonya. Put the blade down off to the side of tub. We need to talk. Just you and me. Ok?" Maybe that is too direct but it works. She still looks confused but manages to drop the blade on the side of the tub for the time being.

I reach for the blade and put it on the sink counter away from her. She is shaking in terror and shock so I need to get her out of the tub. Now this is where it gets tricky. I don't believe she really

16

trusts me. Who in their right mind would trust a complete stranger who shows up out of nowhere in the same room as one is about to off themselves? But, Tonya is not in her right state of mind. I grab the towel off the rack and hand it to her, in a gentlemanly fashion of course.

I stare at her and tell her very specifically, "Look. I am going out and will be sitting in the living room. You dry yourself off and puts some clothes on. When you are ready to come out to the living room, please do so. Take your time."

I stare into her eyes and they say it all. She is not as fearful as she was earlier and her brain is telling her to make better decisions. The first being to trust me, I hope. I crack a smile to her and she relaxes a bit. I start to exit the bathroom via the door this time but turn around immediately as I forget to ask her something just as she is standing up. Whoops. Sorry about that. But you do have an interesting tattoo located, well, located in not a normally visible spot. I guess I wasn't supposed to see it.

"Sorry, but do you have anything to drink?" I start to ask her but then think I should probably go find it myself and close the door behind me. Rather quickly.

I hear a huge sigh from the other side of the door. I think to myself that at least she is still breathing and I head off to the living room.

I find the barren cabinet she calls a bar. There is some Firewater, some sweet Vermouth, some cheap-flavored vodka and way in the back, probably not hers, is some white label whiskey bottle. I take my chances on the white label stuff versus the way too-sweet vodka junk. I start to pour her a drink, as I can only assume she needs one right about now but think the better of it. I am not her boyfriend, hell I am not even her friend. She doesn't even know my name. We will keep my name under wraps for the time being.

I stroll over to the living room and check out the books on the bookcase. As I scan the various titles, there is one that strikes my fancy. It is called *Tequila Highway: Last Exit*. Wow, I will have to ask about that one. I continue pacing about the living room. I think it would be rude to start watching TV or go searching for a baseball game. I don't know how much time she needs to face me, the one who stopped her from killing herself. She is going to be a little reserved about it for a while. At least I don't feel she is in danger anymore but this isn't an exact science either. I can hear drawers opening and closing so at least she is moving about.

I finish my drink but cling to the glass for security. It gives me something to keep me occupied until the next phase of tonight's show: the confrontation and why I am here. I think about what to say to her before I hear the bedroom door open and she walks out wearing a nice, sleek sleeveless top and a red skirt. Ok, I get caught gazing at her, not realizing she is dressed to go out instead of moping around the apartment. It certainly caught me off guard, but, at least I can get a better drink in town.

She stops in front of me. I say nothing. What can I say, I am speechless and she knows it. Instead, she takes the lead.

"Hello, my name is Tonya and I am your blind date tonight." She is nervous but delivers her line perfectly.

I give her a name she can call me for now. She accepts it but knows I am not telling her everything.

"Obviously, you know more about me and seen more of me...... I would like to get outta here and go get something to eat. Do you have plans already or is that acceptable?"

"I am perfectly fine with that. I trust your decision on the food option as I am not from around here."

"Excellent because we need to head downstairs and wait for our ride." She checks her phone. "We have about 6 minutes before the Uber taxi arrives to pick us up."

I think I am going to like this Tonya. I feel really good about stopping a potential tragedy and turning it around to something grand. The beginning of a wonderful relationship with my new friend.

I turn toward the door before I feel the tug of her hand on my shoulder. I spin around to face her and she plants a kiss on my cheek. She then whispers in my ear which gives me a warm sensation throughout my body, "Thank you for what you did. I owe YOU for......everything."

In moments like this, there are the certain actions I call "perks of the job" and thus I say a silent thanks for the special gift that was bestowed upon me to help another human. In this case, to save Tonya.

Tonya and I grow ever closer over the next few weeks. We aren't exactly the normal couple in young love but more like the best of friends. I give some, very limited mind you, details of what transpired to lead me to her apartment on that particular night. She eventually did seek out some counseling which helped her to move past the original issues plaguing her.

I can't say that I didn't caused some pain and discomfort to the man that caused Tonya to nearly take her own life. I guess I will be judged in the end so I may have one or two minor blemishes on my record. Besides, he was an asshole and had it coming. Now he is marked with a reputation that you can't cover up and every woman in this town knows about it. Justice served.

It is also interesting to note that during this time, Tonya and I decide to go into business together. More like a partnership, to keep others from making the bad decisions or stupid mistakes that they may regret later in life. It really is all her idea. I setup the shell company and provide the financing, also a little perk of the "gift" when played right and not too illegal. Well, maybe illegal, but it's all for the benefit of the greater good. Besides, the people that I acquired the financing from, well taking without repaying, probably will not be filing a police report. Everyone wins and nobody innocent gets hurts. Yeah, rack up another blemish on my record.

Within six months from our chance encounter and first meeting, we pack up her stuff and move her and myself to Las Vegas. We finalize the charter for a corporation and procure a really swinging office in one of the major casinos and then finally started to line up clients. In Las Vegas, the clientele pool is much bigger than we initially anticipated. It starts to feel like a 9-5 job but we are not in it for the money. I can inject funds at any time to keep the corporation going. But, the money keeps flowing in, legally, and we realize that we should expand and hire more people.

At first, Tonya is upset as she enjoyed this special thing between only me and her. She enjoyed the stable working relationship and professionalism we maintain through the day. However, in the off hours she loves to be wined and dined at a fancy restaurant along the Strip or at the shared house we keep on the north end of town.

We never defined our 'relationship' or 'status' and keep it clean most of the time. We maintain separate bedrooms but answer the occasional "call" when the alcohol flowed too freely on a particular night or when one (or both) of us have the urge to qualm a biological issue.

Still, I always feel that she will go through her life knowing that she always 'owes me' or something to the effect. I never tell her that she will have to say good-bye to me as I will be leaving in less than a year or so. She will be devastated and I hope she can recover from my eventual departure. I would never leave her empty-handed, however, in regard to being financially established. The emotional strain will be another matter though.

As I began to feel it some time ago, it becomes quite clear to me to seek out the one to replace me in Tonya's life. During the nights that she thinks I am retired for the evening, I am actually following the vibes to track down the next one whose life I am destined to change. I also hope to stumble upon a person who may fill in for me, though, I can never be replaced. I can't help but feel those thoughts of how Tonya's life has been altered because of me. In my searching, I need to find the person that will have a profound influence in both Tonya's and my own life. This is what ultimately leads me to Lisa entering the picture.

I track down and find Lisa even before I figured out what she was going to be in the grand scheme of things. Lisa had the all the makings of a happy and destined life: good schooling, post-secondary education, supportive social structure and so on. So why would she come about on my radar, you may ask? Well, just because one has everything lined up for a positive future does not necessarily mean their future will end up positive. This was the tragic case for Lisa.

Tonya agreed with me that we should hire more staff. Also, it was thrown into the discussion to just sell the business and retire to a Caribbean Island but we both knew deep down it would never work out. Tonya knew the barriers that prevented us from having a "normal" relationship, unfortunately, that we could never have one. She also shared in the secret, as I told no one else, about the fact that I will become mortal and die one day. I think this scared her more than anything, I have become the most normal and stable thing she has had in her life in a very long time.

The day finally came. Tonya was positioned at the front desk as people enter from the double doors. I had a private office to give an authoritative effect and the view was spectacular overlooking the town. Adjacent to my office, we had a waiting area, comfortably outfitted with a plush sofa that shared the fabulous view of the Vegas Strip.

I remember the day Lisa walked into our office and into our lives. It forever altered how Tonya viewed me, how she spoke to me, and even how she looked at me. Oh sure, the love was always there, but when Lisa entered the picture, I sensed a change in Tonya. It was probably better this way. She had to learn to live without me.

Lisa approached Tonya's desk and sat on the edge. Pretty edgy to say the least but Tonya held her poker face tightly.

"You must be Lisa," Tonya asked, not fazed by the cavalier attitude of this brash female right in front of her.

"I am Lisa and I am ready to start." She scans Tonya both to see what level of influence this female has and, more importantly, who she has to speak with to get the job.

Tonya quickly has enough of this woman's arrogance for the time being and escorts her to the sofa to await the appointment with me. In hindsight, I laugh realizing that Tonya and Lisa will fast become the best of friends. It is sad that a certain event has to transpire to bring these two women together but, as we all know, it is usually a crisis that brings people together.

I watch Tonya as she escorts Lisa to the sofa and I wink covertly to Tonya as she returns to her desk. I decide to sit down on the sofa to have a chat with Lisa just to see how candid she can be when the scenario changes.

"Oh hello, do you mind if I join you?" I innocently ask, hoping she doesn't pick up that I am the one who will be interviewing her.

My presence doesn't faze her and her poise never falters. She judges me to be a non-influential, non-threat, unless she assumes I am interviewing as well. She still but warily gives me the once over looking for a briefcase or something else that would denote another interviewee.

I watch her closely, studying her reactions, and, more importantly, picking up her energy to see if it is good vibrations or bad. I sense only the good, nothing bad whatsoever. She passed the first test.

Lisa chats with me amicably, instead of sitting in awkward silence or staring out the window toward the Vegas Strip. "So, are you here for an interview?" she asks but then adds the more challenging question. "Why are you applying here?'

Hmmmm. Now this is interesting. She cuts straight to the chase. No feigning interest and idle chit-chat, but rather she is interested in what motivates me to be here. Fascinating, to say the very least. She clearly assumes she will be hired, yet questions why there are others here to compete against her. I must throw a curveball back at her to keep her guessing.

"Lisa, what drives you to want to work here?"

Startled that I addressed her by her name, and then clearly rationalizing that I am the interviewer, she answers cheekily, "Well, we would not be having this conversation otherwise."

I remember head-hunting her back in Chicago under a different name and email whilst I was on a call during all the shootings in the city in the summertime. Some of my *colleagues* were quicker to the draw and left me with little to do. I vividly heard the cries, recalling in my mind, every once in a while, shootings tend to leave a longer mark in my memory. That was when I stumbled upon a faint, yet audible cry in the night to which I responded to right away. I thought I would solve her issue by 'offering her an interview for a job' in the company with the help of an associate posing as an employment headhunter hence the fake name and email. He gave her the instructions and eventually paid for her flight and lodging for the interview here in Las Vegas. Only then did I realize her fate was somewhat different. At the time, I felt I made the right decision, but, in the end, it might prove to be a fatal mistake.

I knew right away she was the perfect fit for our little company. It's too bad the most important decision will not come for about four months hence, but, I will savor the joyous moments for now. I call over to Tonya and she already has poured the champagne and we all toast to good fortune and welcoming Lisa to the team. Why spoil a good thing when I don't have to? Still, I knew secretly it would be a difficult dilemma and I sometimes question what's the value of it all. Was it worth it, despite knowing what the outcome will be? I like to think I made the right decision in spite of all that I know what will transpire.

"Lisa, how does it feel to part of something new, something so……. Tonya, what is the word I am looking for?"

She pours a little more vino in my glass, "Exhilarating?"

I clink Lisa's glass first and peer over to Tonya, giving her a nod of affirmation. Tonya has always been privy to many of the things I hold most dear. Now, we work out a way to indoctrinate Lisa in the ways of the company and the corporate culture.

The first few months were fun and happy. We all worked well as a team and we never really viewed it as work or drudgery. It was more like hanging out with friends at a beach house over the long weekend. The clients were steady and Lisa administered the checking in process and the appointments which left Tonya able to elevate to client prep and, myself, out marketing for new clients when not consulting the established clients.

I never thought Lisa had any inkling as to the truth or the real reason why the clients were here or what service we really provided. I know of *colleagues* who have similar set-up's and it has proven to be an efficient system if not quite profitable. I even had a few visit my office on occasion and take notes. I should have franchised the system, now that I think about it.

It was around the fifth month that Lisa started showing signs of complacency and yearning to do something more. Maybe she had this vision of a dream job and every aspect has been answered: generous pay and benefits, relaxed working environment, flexible schedule, and even an account with the casino we were housed in. I knew in my heart it was something different. Tonya's thoughts on the matter leaned more toward Lisa feeling like the third wheel. Maybe I will have to sort out what mine and Tonya's status might be someday. Today is not that day though.

Lisa was shutting down for the day and locking up the clients' documents and closing the front door. She was the last to join the after-action activity as I like to call it, where the three of us kick back with a drink in hand on the comfy sofa looking out the window. It has been nearly five months since Lisa joined the company yet there has not been one day that goes by that the three of us haven't embarked in our daily ritual.

It is quite amazing and I still get a kick out of gazing upon The Strip with all the craziness out there each and every day. We also use this time to wind down and chat away, usually non-work, non-sports, and non-weather topics. A genuine free-flowing discussion amongst friends that evolved into something better than the "so how was your day dear?"

Tonya was already cozying away on a white wine, South African vintage. I myself have my bourbon neat in one hand with some salty pretzels in the other. Not to be out done and wanting to impress us with her two-week intensive bartending school degree, Lisa makes herself a gin and tonic. She then sits down next to me...too close for comfort, like we are on a date close. Tonya almost spits out her wine, apparently choking on it while trying hard not to laugh. I wait for the opportunity to stick out my tongue toward Tonya when Lisa was otherwise looking down and adjusting herself.

"Hey Lisa. Tonya and I were just discussing where to hold the next company conference. Any suggestions? So far, the submissions have been: Cancun; Bahamas; Geneva, Switzerland; and a rather unique request for Seoul, Korea." Even I found it hard not to snicker from reading the made-up list.

Lisa takes a long sip from her drink and contemplates her answer.

Seriously, Tonya and I were only joking and said it in jest.

Lisa takes another drink before responding in a calm tone. "Let me ask you two a serious question."

"Shoot. Go ahead," Tonya and I say together.

"You two are much older than me and I have assumed both of you have traveled far and wide."

Tonya's face grimaces as she thinking that she is not that much older than Lisa.

We both nods our heads. She doesn't know the half of it but I am getting a strange vibration the more she talks.

Lisa presses on, "I want to visit all those places and more. I want to do it now. I feel I have an opportunity to do it but I am so very appreciative for what you all have given me with this company."

I close my eye for a second. I see in focus what I blew off earlier when I first came across Lisa. In my mind, the vision of Lisa's future is so vivid to me as it becomes so clear in my mind. I see her traveling to Europe. I see all her hikes, her exploring European cities and then I see her murdered in Prague. I snap out of my vision and shake violently. I try to cough as to feint it was my drink going down the wrong pipe. Lisa stops her traveling monologue and Tonya rushes to my side patting me on the back. We look into each other's eyes and Tonya knows exactly what I am thinking and the concern overcomes her. She fights the tears as she sees it in my eyes: Lisa's death.

I regain my composure and Tonya returns to her seat. We played it off and hid our doubts but continue listening to the joys of Lisa's future plans to travel the world, starting with Europe. She talks of the money she has saved to afford this sojourn. She mentions how much time she has looked forward to exploring, and she discusses some people she has lined up to embark on this journey with. It was that very moment where Tonya and I felt like the concerned parents listening to their child talk about going away to the State University in the fall. I felt helpless and stood by as Lisa spilled out the final plan, *for her own demise.* After the one drink, she bids adieu and heads off into the night.

Tonya and I only stare at each other. I can feel the hatred Tonya has for me building up deep inside her. I refresh our drinks but she leaves her glass on the table never reaching for it. The cold eyes look in my direction and after a long, drawn out silence she finally formulates exactly what to say to me. I guessed it would be summed up in three words.

"How could you?" I guessed correctly.

"You have no idea, do you?"

"I would like to think I am starting to know you better than most people. After all, you did *save me once*." Tonya starts to cry but continues, "Why are you not saving her. You know perfectly well she is going to *die* on this trip."

I did not want to correct Tonya in telling her that Lisa is going to be murdered on this trip but it is a moot point. Tonya now knows if we let Lisa go and travel, we will never see her alive again. I take another sip of my bourbon as I stare out toward the Stratosphere hotel.

"You cold-hearted bastard." Tonya leaves the office slamming the door shut.

I block out the screams and wails I experienced ages ago. I remember hearing these sounds when I first saw Lisa in Chicago but I chose to ignore them back then. I now understand as they have come to full fruition, in the oddest of coincidences, or maybe it was fate, however one wants to view it. Was Lisa going to die no matter what or was it my intervention that ultimately will cause her death?

Now this is not part of the perks package of the job. Here I know Lisa is going to die, yes she will be murdered, if she goes on this trip to Europe. She has it set in her head that she is going on this trip no matter what. I could intervene and demand she not go but what point what that be?

It is about choice: we choose this path or that path. One could either play it safe all their life or take a chance. The tricky part is what causes the bad decision: the playing it safe or the taking a chance. Ha ha - the cosmic irony. People always assume the playing it safe is the "safer" or good decision and the "taking a chance" is the gutsy or bad decision. But that is not always the case.

Unfortunately, I understand all of this but don't want to explain it to Tonya or Lisa. Yeah, it's not going to work with either of them. For Tonya, I have to tell her Lisa has always been fated to die whether in Chicago or Prague, it makes no difference. It was already decided by someone higher up than me. As for Lisa, I will wish her well and tell her to be safe. She is just unlucky to die at such an early age. It is what it is, that's life or in this case, death.

I open my eyes and rise up from my couch. I walk to the door, taking a look back before turning out the light. I open the door, step out and shut the door locking it in the process. I take a deep breath and pick up where Tonya is in the casino. I sort out her vibes immediately and head down to her, to console her on the decision that is already made.

There was much joy and fanfare and Lisa's last day of work. We throw a big party and invite many people to wish her well on her journeys and experiences she is about to encounter. She takes a moment to approach us at one point during the celebrations in the office.

She grabs me on the shoulder and pulls me closer to her. She whispers those words that I will never forget. "I really thought you would try to stop me. Thank you for believing in me and supporting me. I will never forget you. You are the sole reason I am doing this." Wow I am not sure if I should be happy for those words or feel like she just "coupe de grace" me in the heart. I beam at her as if she were my own daughter. Although I do wish she would have made a different decision, a different choice.

"Lisa, you are correct. I was going to stop you. Instead, I give you this."

Lisa looks confused by my words.

I stuff an envelope containing a lot of cash into her hands. Her confused look turns to embarrassment and she starts to cry as she takes the cash gift.

I recover the awkward scene by giving words of caution. "Be safe and always have us in your thoughts as we do you!" It was the only thing I could muster without being too emotional and shed a tear of my own.

Lisa then turns to Tonya and they exchange kind words to one another. Tonya cannot hold back anymore and begins to cry out loud. It starts a chain reaction as Lisa cries out too. I think a few of the guests cry out of sympathy as well.

Tonya and Lisa let go of one another and the party continues. Eventually, everyone leaves and we say our last good-byes to Lisa. We never forget the last look on her face, the look of contentment and pure happiness.

We close the office for two weeks. Tonya and I needed time off and we go traveling around the area, approximately a 500-mile radius, seeing the beautiful national parks of the West. We talk about this and that as we hike this park, see this wonderful sight, or eat at such and such restaurant in whatever random city. We decide at some point to return to our working lives and just start to receive the first of many post cards from our world traveler, Lisa, writing about her travels and adventures.

Months went by and our lives continued forward. Then it happened one night. I felt it so strongly and will never forget it. Apparently, I have some unique bond with Lisa that cannot be explained. I could hear Tonya rushing from her bedroom and opening the door. I was already sitting up with the sad yet emotionless expression about my face. Tonya never made it to the bed but instead collapses right there on the bedroom floor. She screams out in sorrow and I try to comfort her the best I can but it isn't good enough. In my mind, I think Tonya blames me for Lisa's death. I may not have been the one who pulled the trigger but I feel she blames me for killing Lisa. If she were a jury, she would render her verdict guilty to me for causing the death of Lisa. Court adjourned and no appeal.

Except, I leave. I left the house without recourse or purpose. I jump from city to city with destination unknown. I just fly, rest, fly and continue this pattern until I stop at some small town with an equally small-town bar. I go into the bar, a stranger among the local crowd, and sit down at a bar stool toward the end of the bar. Some patrons recognize the 'look' and decide not to bother this stranger. The bartender tends to my needs without asking to many questions. I throw two twenty dollar bills and bartender simply acknowledges and refills the glass. He even brings by and drops off some pretzels.

I stare forward. Not looking at anything really, just staring. Could I have prevented Lisa's death like I did for Tonya? Would it have mattered, really? I mean if I prevented Lisa from going to Europe and ultimately dying there, would she have just died here in some freak bus accident? Or would it have been something more gruesome? The bartender refills the glass and collects the money sitting in front of me. This is what happens when I try to live a 'normal life' i.e. 9-5 job, with a girlfriend or whatever Tonya is, and a house in the suburbs. This was a reminder that I was not the normal, human guy any more. I was something different and I should start acting like it.

This means only one thing. I down the last shot of whiskey in the glass and tap my fingers to the bartender telling him to keep the change. He nods his head in agreement and watches me as I exit the bar. I decide to get back on my high horse and tell Tonya things are going to be different. For one, I need to leave her for an undetermined amount of time.

Tonya is more perceptive than I originally thought. When I return to the house, I find her on the telephone discussing plans to visit her folks back East. She is also multi-tasking on the computer booking airline tickets. Ah, that's my dear, efficient to the last. I hope you remember to use your frequent flyer card to rack up those air miles. She notices me but with the balancing act she is performing, she merely smiles to acknowledge I have returned to our shared domicile.

I grab a beer and go outside to sit in the temperate Las Vegas evening. I really see the stars out tonight and begin to relax as the evening converts to night. The sliding door opens 15 minutes later and Tonya comes out to join me. She does not speak a word but, rather, grabs my hands and holds them tight. I break the silence by almost breaking my empty beer bottle on the glass table. The sound echoed too loudly in the otherwise quiet and peaceful night.

She turns her head toward me. "Sorry, I was on the phone with my folks. I am going to visit them in two days. That was the earliest I could book a plane ticket. I was hoping we could…." She stops cold in her thought.

I wrestle my hands free from hers. "We could *what*....?"

I see the expression about her face. She is stomaching enough courage to deal with me but she is ready to explode. I see her emotions waging war with one another. Should she stay or should she go? What will become of us when she returns? If she ever returns?

I reach for her hand this time and take it, squeezing it tight like I did on the first night we met each other. I hear her breathe heavily. I pause for a moment to choose the words carefully. "Tonya, I will be doing some traveling as well. This break will do us some good and then we will talk.... Later at some point." I suspect the later may never come to fruition but I still lean over to kiss her on the forehead as to signify the sealing of the pact, the committed agreement between the two of us.

She squeezes my hand in affirmation and we sit outside for a period of time, not saying anything, simply staring off at the nighttime skyline together. We enjoy the sacred moment together, in silence, as this will be one of our last solemn times together.

The next day, we close up the office and hang a sign that reads "Owners taking a long-needed vacation." We leave an even wittier answering machine message and lock up the doors. We head down to the casino manager's office and pre-pay for two months' rent, figuring that would buy us some time to do what we each have to do. The manager was happy to collect the rent but sad to see us gone for such a long time. He offers us a drink with him on the house at one of the casino bars. How could we decline? When a casino offers you anything free, you take it while you can.

The next day, I drive Tonya to the airport. It really is a noble act though I could have transported her to her destination just as easy another way, my way, in less time. Since the time I have been with her, I have been less inclined to demonstrate my 'gifts or talents' in front of her. I think I have been humanizing myself when I am with her. I supposed this was not a bad thing but it will be time soon enough to show my true colors once again. Despite the show of power and limitless travel via my way, she much prefers the traditional and 'normal human' way to travel across the country in an airplane. I sit with her at the gate until she hears the announcement for her flight and boards with her First-Class ticket in hand.

It is likely this will be the last time I see her. She doesn't think of it but in my mind, I know this is the last meeting between the two of us. What a complete 360 degree change I have witnessed in this woman. From our first encounter to this very minute, I have begun to realize the true meaning of some of those haunting questions that often start *what if*. I simply hug her, no, embrace her with all my might nearly crushing her and for the first time, actually showing some human emotion. She responds in kind and gives me a passionate kiss that makes saving her life mean so much to me at this very moment. I will never forget her eyes and the way she glanced at me one last time before turning her head and walking out of sight, and out of my life forever.

I turn and disappear in the blink of an eye. I am back and now I am traveling on to New Orleans. The Big Easy. It is time to cue the jazz band to play for I will be throwing it down on Bourbon Street tonight. Oh yeah, the Saints will be marching in, with a Hurricane drink in hand.

I coolly arrive, touching down on Bourbon St in a wink of an eye. Nobody notices my sudden appearance or they are too drunk and decide to not think of what they might, or might not, have seen. And who cares? The merriment and foolishness will continue on and into the night. Hence, I jump right in the action and grab some incredible Cajun food to start things off.

I stroll into the first place I come across, aptly named the Cajun House, and walk up to the counter to place an order. Gumbos, jambalayas, creole this and that, the mind could explode with all the tasty choices. I ended up ordering two different entrees and happily sit down in anticipation of the feast.

This was an open-air place and the doors were wide open, most likely a blessing in this stifling humidity. Which is cool, in the literal sense, as I get to watch the people outside walking past in all the craziness. It is fun and there was certainly the fill of bizarre and fun-loving party-goers. I turn my head back for a split second to see if a waiter is bringing my food and then look back toward the street. It was kinda creepy to feel her staring at me from the street. Of course, one will argue that she was looking inside the place as a potential place to dine as I am about to do...if my food ever gets delivered. On the other side of the argument, one could say that her gesturing exactly to me by pointing her finger in my direction would probably win the argument.

I was kinda taken aback by this stranger's gesture to me. Though I was looking at her, well, staring more likely at this point I wasn't really looking at her. I mean I could not describe anything about her other than she was a woman and she was walking next to some dude. Oh, and she was wearing a shirt, but, I can't even recall the color. See what I mean?

Normally, I would have brushed it off to drunken flirtatious actions. However, the more disturbing part was the voice inside my head (remember, the cries of people in various degrees of pain or hurt when I turn on the gift) was completely silent during the whole finger-pointing episode. In all my years, I've never encountered something like that. It was as though she had a talent to block out all the voices. I wish she would have developed the technology to block people from yakking on their phones in public places but that's a different issue. This woman is certainly unique and I will be seeing her again, I can almost bet on it. Well, at least my food has arrived and I dig right in. Yes, it is delicious and I start to forget about the woman who gave me the the the finger, literally, minutes ago.

After the food, I went to acquire a French Quarter mainstay. No not beignets but hand grenades. You know, the green melon drink in the long green plastic tube you see a lot of folks toting around. It is much easier to drink and carry around one of these and have it refilled at various locations than to try to carry around a Hurricane glass. You see my point?

As I was drinking from one, I watched a jazz band play away from the cheap seats (aka the street view). The bouncers were not bothering people to move along or come inside to watch with a 2-drink minimum. I was so into the music at that moment in time, I never saw her bump into me nearly spilling her drink all over me. I regained my street smarts and figured she was trying to pickpocket me but lucky for me, I carry my wallet in the front pocket and not the back. I used to keep a dummy/fake wallet in the back with a dollar in it along with a note that said *sucker.* Except the wallet kept getting stolen and, once, one pickpocketer actually tracked me down and tried to punch me out. Some people have no sense of humor at all.

I reached for my front wallet to ensure its safety while trying to avoid the spilling beer and catching the female from falling over her own clumsiness or drunkenness. And, in the moment, I felt her. No, not the feeling of her, but of something *weird* coming from her. I felt her cries and pain for a second and then it disappeared or was blocked immediately. I released her about the time the equally drunk male was realizing the fact that a strange man was holding his woman. She steadies herself and he quickly wraps his arm around her for support, clearly staking his claim she was a "hands off zone." So much for trying to help keep her from falling face first on the dirty Bourbon Street pavement.

I start to walk away, feeling I have done enough in this situation but I feel a hand, more feminine than masculine, and slowly turn around to hear the drunken-speech coming from her. Her man has moved on to drinking from his hand grenade tube leaving her to do what she felt needs to be done.

Amidst the noise of the crowd and tons of people on the street, "Thank you. I would...I would like to buy youse a drink." She stammered, nearly spilling her own drink in the process. Clearly she needs another drink, I thought wryly.

"Sure." It's great to have a woman, well, anyone buy me a drink in this town.

We head over to this place across the street and it is about half-filled inside. We all grab a table toward the back. The band on stage just finished their set and were taking a break along with passing the bucket around for tips. I haven't heard them play a song yet I felt compelled to throw a couple bucks in the bucket only because it gets rid of them faster.

The guy, I think he said his name was Sid, went to the bar to get a round of drinks. He didn't even bother asking what I wanted. I assumed he had done this before as he obliges to his wife and her 'making new friends,' buy them a drink, and see you later routine.

"What's your name?" I give her my name and ask her in kind for hers.

"Fiona." She says spiting beer when speaking the first syllable. "You wanna dance?"

I look at her thinking I am being played. "What about your husband?"

"Oh him? I don't think you want to dance with him." With that she takes my hand and we go on the dance floor. We dance. Sid walks by with the drinks and sits at the table playing on his phone and not bothered one iota. Fiona and I dance like crazy drunken folks.

We go back to the table and drink away toasting to not working, people I don't know, and just about anything else. I had a moment when a mother and daughter pair entered the bar, right before the band started back up and they danced along to the DJ dance music. I start to think about the mother and daughter as they danced away the hour. Maybe I drank too much and felt guilt for Tonya and Lisa. Maybe I should be thinking about my new friends, Sid and Fiona, and buy this round of drinks. I think the alcohol is starting to catch up with me.

We have some more laughs, dances and drinks before the wee hours of early morning stumble upon us. For whatever reason, we go walking about the town. We pass the church and cut thru Jackson Square. We cross the street and yak away talking about everything and nothing. We cross the tracks and head toward the mighty Mississippi River and sit along the banks. The air was chilly and smell of the River surrounded us. We stare at the great river and gaze off to the night skyline.

I felt so relaxed and so content. I have no worries and life was going great at the moment. Here is a couple who seem happy with each other and perfectly accepting me, as the third wheel, on their night out.

Now - everything started to get weird after this point.

Fiona is sitting next to me on the bench looking at the river. Sid is standing off to the side as if playing the point man. Fiona stands up and walks toward my front, facing me. She puts her hands together over her head and clasps them together once.

I felt the pain immediately. I went from smiling to being in pain in less than the time it took to tell you. She claps her hands together again and I feel the pain, pain I have never felt before. In all the years, I feel afraid for the first time.

I stare at her and try to get a read on her. Nothing. I mean zilch.... nada....no emotion, no pain, no suffering, no nothing. I have never gotten a zero reading on someone.... ever. Now Sid, he is a basket case, and is carrying more emotion than any mortal man. Hmmm, now that I think about it, maybe Fiona is not mortal. Maybe she is like me. I start to say something to her but she already acts.

Fiona shouts, "OK Sid, shoot him."

I thought this was weird to hear it as I am immortal.

The gun fires at my chest grazing the fourth rib and a second shot is fired landing near the first round.

I stop to laugh because I am feeling pain. I peer down and see blood trickling out from my shirt. Well, that's weird. Why am I bleeding?

Fiona is grinning at me. She lunges forward and her face is next to mine. "You have no idea who I am, do you? You don't remember at all, do you?"

I am filled with confusion, mixed emotions, voices in my head and now blood seeping out of my chest and onto my shirt.

My eyes are filled with loss. My body reaps of pain and suffering. However, my soul is now at peace.

"You know what happens next." Those were the last words I heard as I lose consciousness and slump forward. I gaze upon the Mississippi River flowing on by as one of my last visions. I silently say a prayer and my last good-bye to Tonya before I drop dead, finally after all these years. Not immortal anymore.

TIME OF WHITE

You are not gonna believe this.

I think I finally did *him* justice. It took me many months and a lot of time spent but I am closing in on them. You know the ones who ended *his* life. Now comes the tricky part: how to kill them both and finish this once and for all? Will it exact the revenge that I have sought after for so long? And, what will happen to me afterwards? Will I be just as bad as them? You know what, I don't care anymore.

God, I miss *him* so much. I never quite understood *him* but after having so many lonely nights thinking about what we had, I feel that I should have, could have, might have done it better. I think about the time I spent with *him* in Las Vegas and cherish all those memories we shared together. And yes, I forgive *him* for the whole Lisa situation and realize a lot of things about that whole circumstance now. It was such an eye-opening experience and I get it, finally. I know *he* can hear me. I bet *he* is laughing at me. I miss *his* laugh. I can see *him* sporting a big ole grin for what I have turned out to be. Especially since I have become what *he* once was.

Ok, I found them. Here they come. It is time for some revenge, my way. It is rather amazing to think what has happened to get me to this point.

It was one of the worst times in my life. People always reminisce about how they would love to go back in time to re-live their 20's. Not me and certainly I would have chosen to forget most of it.

Well, except for the time when I met *him* rather abruptly late one night but I am jumping the gun.

Ok Ok. First things first. I was once of those girls in high school that had all the popularity, no not for *that* reason, but was rather liked by many because I was likeable. Though thinking back, I was not thought too highly of by the school administration as my grades were not exactly stellar or Mensa material. I did not care back then and played it this way well into my early 20's. I was hoping I would do this and that and maybe something would happen eventually or somebody would come along and, *voila*, easy street for me.

Years later, I started watching people around me graduating from university or starting their entry-level careers. Worst yet, some were starting to have whining, crying babies. Everyone one around me was succeeding or starting to form their own path to success and a happy life. Well, I was not gonna get knocked up at the tender age of 23 and, one day, I reflected back wondering what I had accomplished in the last five years after high school graduation. Cue in the cricket chirping in the background.

Have I put you to sleep yet? Are you tired of hearing about somebody who did nothing with their life and is now complaining about it? Do I look upset because I chose the career path of a waitress first and then moved up to bartender extraordinaire? A damn good one at that, just for the record. Come on down to the bar sometime. But remember the rules. One, order something simple like a draft beer or a bottle beer. Maybe a straight shot of some whiskey is ok, I suppose. Two, please stop hitting on me. I have heard every fathomable pick-up line, direct or indirect, from every male and even from a few females too. I did think twice about the females as they were cuter than most of the guys that tried their luck with the lame pick-up lines. Seriously people, do I go to your workplace and try to hit on you while you are busy doing your job?

While we are on the subject, here's another thought. Instead of hitting on me, try hitting the tip jar. You may even get a smile or a sassy wink from me but you sure as hell ain't getting my phone number, email, key to my apartment or whatever. You should be so lucky that your beer isn't lukewarm or mixed drink isn't watered down.

You are probably starting to wonder if I even like guys at all. Well, I do love the ones that tip generously. I love the ones who order a beer, yeah, a simple beer without fruit in a bottle with no glass. I especially love the ones with a woman as they don't try to make small talk with me. I didn't have the time or the patience for a relationship, not in my line of work.

It was quite a surprise the day I met Steve. *Yeah yeah, I know I can't believe she fell for some pickup line after all though the pickup line was actually a good one!* I actually met Steve in a nightclub on my day off when I was with Susie and Maria. We decided to go for Italian meal and the then head off to a new night club, call TRAXX, to let loose and dance. I thought it would be great to get out and socialize with my friends before they moved on and started having babies or real jobs.

The meal was fine but not worth mentioning but I'll tell you anyways. I had some chicken & pasta dish and it was ok. It was more interesting to hang out with my friends and let someone else wait on us for a change. Who cares if the chicken was bland or the pasta sauce was a little cold. The bottles, yes bottles, of red wine went down rather well. I do remember that part. However, it turned out to be an unforgettable night or one I want to forget months later.

So here we are. Three sassy ladies dressed to kill, figuratively, though some lads we walked past appeared to have heart attacks as we swished on by past them. Hey, if they wanted to talk to us and buy us a drink, then they should be older or wealthier, preferably both. That's the way it is as I didn't want to tend bar all my life. Also, I heard the tips start decreasing for a female bartender after the age of 27 and time will be running out for me in a few years.

We head over to TRAXX nightclub and see there is a long line to get in the place. Apparently, the word has gotten out that this is the place to be or be seen, as least for this week. It doesn't matter to me. It's a "perk" of my line of work – you know, a quid pro quo kind of thing.

Let me elaborate. If I happen to know a certain guy who is a bouncer at a particular club, then I will more than likely give him a drink or two 'on the house' when he is ordering a drink at my place of work on his night off. Likewise, if said bouncer is working a particular Saturday nightclub and it is my night off, I would walk up to him and say, "Hello Tom" and hug him. In this industry, we forge alliances taking advantage of the system as much as we possibly can. If the police officers can get free coffee and donuts, then bar workers should get free drinks and free admission in nightclubs.

Tom recognizes me right away, "Well, hello Tonya. You and your friends are looking super fine tonight. Did you want to tear up the dancefloor now or wait until I get off at 2am and we can do some serious partying?"

I laugh at his ruse. I know he is kidding are at least I think he is. I still rub his hair and slowly glide my hand down his unshaven face. He flinches, but only because he loses his tough-guy bouncer persona for a second.

"Go on in. I will call you on my day off for payback." He replies and then fends off the barbs from the ones in the front of the line waiting to go in.

The three of us saunter thru the doors like we are celebrities or something. We might as well work it while we can. I brush past him telling him to call me sometime but Tom just smiles back at me. He can't call me as he doesn't have my phone number. He knows it and I know it. We play the charade of solidarity for the bar-workers of America. The perks of the miserable career choice.

Susie heads to the bar to mooch a free drink from some unsuspecting male who might think, for a split second, he might actually have a chance with her. Nope. Not this woman. Just pay your 10 bucks for her drink and be happy she glanced at you and touched your shoulder. Move along, your 15 seconds of fame are gone. Susie is already moving on and targeting the next victim for another free drink.

Maria and I love to dance and we love to make everyone in the place stare at us as if we are working for tips. We move out on the dance floor slowly and move and gyrate to the sounds of the current hip-hop songs. We wait for a few songs until we move closer and closer to one another. By then, we have weeded out the ones who think *what the hell I may have a chance* versus the ones who think *those women are out of my league and I am exiting the dancefloor now. Maybe they are still running draft beer specials at the bar.*

After the smoke clears and the playlist changes to a more European techno beat, there are two males who brave their souls to take a chance with Maria and myself. I don't remember the name of the one who put his moves to work with Maria but I do remember the male who picked me out. His name was Steve. Or was it Mr. Asshole which is probably more accurate. Sorry, I should keep to the telling of the events that happened without side commentary. Even if it happens to be true.

For whatever reason that night, I stay on the dance floor with him. Mainly to see if this man, Steve, can woo me enough to follow him to get a free drink or two. I have to admit, he can dance. You'd think he was a professional dancer the way he moved on the dancefloor and without me or his wingman. The wingman is busy putting the moves, unsuccessfully, on Maria. But I am intrigued for whatever reason that night and let him perform his solo moves to the applause of the audience. Hell, these people would have clapped and cheered for anything. I am left there alone to accept his "pitch or pick-up" line after his latest dance performance.

"Come on babe, let's get a drink. I am parched." I always hate when men call me babe but I am thirsty too. I will let it slide this time.

Steve is like Moses and the crowd parts when he strolls forward toward the bar. I am moving quickly to catch up but this 6'3" 220 pounds of solid male is expertly threading his way through the parting throngs of people and I am only too happy to follow along. Maybe ordering the second bottle of red wine at the Italian joint earlier wasn't a good decision after all. I tag along behind like a lost sheep heading to the slaughter. Well, that about sums up what nearly happens down the road.

Steve orders a beer for himself and then turns toward me too but then doesn't ask and instead orders a drink for me. Rather presumptuous on his part but I am drunk, I guess, and keep on rolling with the streak of bad decisions all night. I suddenly realize Susie and Maria absence from my radar but Steve grabs my hand and heads over to a table toward the back, away from the dance floor. I continue to go along like the inebriated sheep I am.

Steve takes me to one of the tables, one that is currently unoccupied in the back of the nightclub. Without hesitation, he commences with a monologue to explain his background, his pedigree and his net worth. These are the sounds any single woman really wants to hear so she can make her informed decision in regard to proceeding forward with the male currently in her vicinity. I take in all that Steve dishes out that night. We formulate the grounds of our relationship by the end of the night. I bought into it all and thought my golden ship had landed and moored up in my port. My life suddenly had a future and it looked pretty easy from this drunken view.

Fast forward. About two months into the relationship with Steve, we started our first of many arguments. He was acting strange over the fact I was going to see my friends, the same friends that I was out with the night I met him. I couldn't rationalize a constructive argument with him and he stormed out of my apartment. He must have thought I should be at his beck and call, anytime, 24-7. I was not that kinda of girl and once he realized that, he got even more neurotic. Or as I like to say, bat-shit crazy but as I was in love and I forgave him every time despite the warnings and pleas from Maria and Susie.

Their first red flags must have been when I started cancelling our girls' night out events. Steve was on my case that week and I just could not deal with his bullshit or the banter from my friends. Some banter from friends is tough to stomach but it is all in good fun. The mental abuse I got from Steve was not fun and it was degrading and it never stopped. When he started, it was a barrage of slings and smartass comments that continued all through into the next week. I was never perfect for him and after a while I started to doubt my self-worth. Why was I even with him and why was he with me? He wanted something better and later I found out he did find a dumbass blonde female that matched his egotistic standards and put up with it. By then, I was last week's trash and he threw me to the curb the very next week.

I was I wreck. I never listened to the advice from my best friends, Susie and Maria, and told them they were wrong and they didn't know the other side of Steve. I defended this bastard to everyone and anything and all for what? For him to damage me so bad that I couldn't take it anymore. I wanted it all to go away. I could not face talking to anyone.

So here is where the whole part of not believing until it is the moment that you do believe. I was never a church-going kind of gal. You have probably guessed that by now. Sure, I knew some people that attended, religiously, every week. I even knew people that talked of faith and God as much as sports and the weather. I was never such a person. I can say my views will be put to the test and it will be changing in the foreseeable future. Sometimes faith is something to believe and sometimes people have to have proof of it all slapped in their face before they get it.

It was the night I found out about Steve and his infidelity. I even heard eventually he lost most of his wealth to bad investing and unwise squandering. See the blonde female he left me for details. It was too late as I was too far gone and honestly felt there was no escape from the dire situation. Can you believe this, all over a guy who jilted me? I was so pathetic back then. It was a miracle that I even survived this long. Except, the real miracle or blessing was about to happen.

I had planned to do it that night. I set the candles out and was beyond the point of no return in my head. I was on a mission and destined to actually go thru with it. I had the newly purchased blade to do it with and had bought some expensive vodka to go out in style. I thought about who would really miss me and decided the list was much shorter than I hoped for. So, it didn't really matter if I was dead or alive, other than to sling beers at the bar down the road. I really had no footprint in this life. The decision was clear to end it and be one less problem in the world.

I ran the bath water and set the candle for the mood. I don't know why I really did that. I drank a fair amount of the vodka and discovered I actually enjoy the taste of decent vodka. Sadly, I figured it out too late in the game as it doesn't matter anymore. I will be dead in less than an hour and won't have the privilege of being a lifelong customer of this brand of vodka. Oh well.

For some reason, I was compelled to do it in the bathtub and naked. I am not sure why naked either. The EMS surely will get a laugh when they have to collect me? Because I feel I came in this world naked and therefore have to go out naked? Maybe because I get to set the mood and tone of the evening. I probably couldn't decide what to wear for the occasion and thus need not worry if my outfit matched. I certainly didn't want to bleed over my green top either as blood is so hard to wash out. Whatever the reason, I will not look very pretty to whoever discovers me in this bathtub days or weeks from after the horrible final act. Yuck, it is disgusting the more I think about it.

With candles burning, I plunge naked into the bathwater complete with bath bubbles. It was fun, after all, and the water was a pretty color from the colorful bath salts. Too bad it will be spoiled with the red blood spewing out of my veins into the tepid water. I'm holding the shiny, new blade in my hand when Fate came by and made a house call. Of all the times, while I was *taking* a bath.

I thought I heard a sound off in the distance earlier. Remembering I live alone with no pets, I assumed it was someone else in the apartment complex. Maybe it was my neighbor bringing home a new 'friend' and he was too drunk to open the door on the first try. Or maybe it was the other neighbor getting ready to go to work. I swear it sounded as though somebody was in my apartment. I supposed it didn't matter as I was going to end it all in a matter of seconds.

Okay. This is the final countdown. Should I start a ten count? Is there a procedure I should do? I guess it is too late to pray. What will happen after I do it? Is it painful? How long will this take? Oh no, am I having second thoughts? I raise my left hand ready to make the first slice into my wrist.

Then *he* appears out of nowhere. I mean literally *out of nowhere*. I start to scream but I am so in shock that I can't formulate in my head what is happening. I double-check to realize I am still holding the blade and I have not, I repeat, I have not made a cut into my clean and smooth wrist.

So, who in hell or heaven is this guy and why is standing there looking at me like I am crazy? Yes, I am a woman and naked in a bathtub, I get that part. But, I was about to kill myself and end it all. Make your pitch stranger, you got about 30 seconds before I will stop responding.

I hear *him* speaking to me. "Hey, how's it going?"

Really? I am about to kill myself and you ask "how's it going?" How do you think it's going? Not good, my friend. Surely you can do better than that. The razor is starting to look better than the direction of this conversation.

I am still in a quandary of killing myself and questioning why this man has suddenly materialized in my bathroom. I even check to make sure I am not already dead. If I survived, I am changing the brand of vodka for the record.

I suddenly realize I am living out the final moments of my pathetic life with a complete stranger watching me. I would have written it differently. I take one more look at him and need to decide if it is now or never. I need not worry about who he is or how he pulled off the really neat appearance in my apartment and the bathroom magic trick.

Then I heard it. I heard him speak my name. Which I never told him.

"Tonya." It was followed by my name spoken a second time.

"Tonya. I am not going to hurt you and I want to help."

I have been making terrible decisions up until this point my whole life. I certainly was one step, well one swipe of the blade, from throwing it all away. From this moment forward, I am making a pact with myself to make better decisions. I will begin by trusting this stranger who mysteriously wants to help me and somehow knows my name. I mean if he cares enough to take time out on a Saturday night to rescue and save me, then he must know something more about the bigger picture. It could be he was just going to rob my apartment after I was dead. Naw, it's got to be better than that, right?

For once in my life, I will trust someone because they are taking an active interest in me. Tonya. Yep that's right. This man is interested in the real Tonya. Perhaps I should make friends with him because he certainly has my back. Still cautious, I hand the blade over to him and, at that moment, truly realize I have been given a second chance to live. Today is my new birthday of living. Oh wait, he has seen me naked as a jaybird and I start to panic again as I feel somewhat vulnerable. He quickly throws me a towel and I proceed to cover up but I am laughing inside, purely out of petty embarrassment.

He speaks a few more things and I hear him and somehow believe him completely. He starts to leave heading into the living room to wait for me. I stand up and start to wrap myself in the towel but he steps back in the bathroom turning to ask something silly. I turn red in embarrassment and twist around inadvertently exposing to him the silly tattoo I had gotten years previously. He actually seems embarrassed now and scampers off quickly out of the bathroom. I sigh in relief. It is refreshing to find a man who cares about me and is not out for his own self-interests or has a dislike for tattooed women.

I contemplate what I am going to do next. As I was going to kill myself, I didn't have any plans for the rest of this evening. I guess I should start making some plans as I need to find out more about this stranger or savior. I get dressed, wearing something nice and order an Uber taxi figuring I am hungry and I definitely should go get something to eat since all I had was some vodka. I might as well invite my new guest as obviously, he is not out to harm me.

I hope he is not disappointed in the limited drink choices in the house as I hear bottles clanging about in the kitchen. I should probably pay for dinner and the drinks tonight. It seems like the right thing to do because I just realized I am now living and not dying, or dead. That is certainly a cause for celebration and the fact that I owe my current living status to this man, the stranger sitting in my living room. I should go out there and entertain my new guest, or maybe learn my new friend's name.

I finish the touch ups on my face to appear presentable to my new friend. I take a deep breath, ready to move out of the old life and start the new one. I exhale and leave the bedroom and the old life behind.

"Hello," I say with renewed confidence.

I continue on, "My name is Tonya and I am your blind date tonight."

He smiles back at me, both relieved and actually happy to be staring at me. Well, that is a good sign. I think he may be attracted to me, an added bonus.

I think about how he must know more about me than he has said plus the fact he has seen my bare ass naked. I can only assume he is not just physically attracted to me but maybe likes my awesome personality Who knows? I try to switch off for now and make it less stressful on my mind as I am embarking in unchartered territory.

I tell him I have already ordered an Uber taxi as we are going out to grab a bite to eat so I can get to know more about him, my blind date. He seems relieved that the itinerary of the evening is already planned. I feel so comfortable around him already and I don't know why. It is a sense of peace and tranquility. I am so digging him now and we haven't even left my apartment.

Out of the blue, I grab his shoulder to turn him around and plant a big fat kiss on his cheek. I don't why but I felt compelled to express my thanks for all that he has done this evening. I tell him I owe him and I remind him I am to pay for dinner tonight, that I won't have a problem with that. He has changed my life so much I can't even comprehend the impact until sometime later. However tonight, we are going to throw down and party all night. I love him already. Thank you, kind stranger as I will never forget you. Promise.

We share a fantastic evening of decent food and good company. We stroll around downtown enjoying the moment and each other. Truth be told, I have never felt so comfortable with anyone else, ever. He seems comfortable as well but I suspect he is holding something back. I don't mean he is married or has a kid in the holding something back. And obviously, the whole appearing in my bathroom at the pinnacle moment certainly needs to be addressed at some point, not tonight though. It is our night tonight, me and *him* and no further questions. Well, there was one issue that first night as he offered to 'take me home'. I did not know what that meant *but I do now.* I opted to take an Uber back and when it arrived, we kissed good night, not good-bye.

We started to establish a communication infrastructure or in other words, we began a daily ritual of text messages and phones calls each and every day. I soon forgot about Steve the jackass and eventually called upon and reignited my friendships with Maria and Susie. I told them I met a new guy who literally saved my life. I did not go on in details but both of them could see the happiness in me and were content with my well-being.

I never told anyone how the events of that particular night transpired, that I almost succeeded in ending it all. Quite frankly, my mental wellness and outlook on life has changed so much I really feel I have no outstanding mental issues. Still, *he* advised I seek a counselor for a few weeks. I did agree to *his* request and graduated from the mental wellness program with flying colors.

Then I saw *him* at my workplace late one night. *He* appeared all of sudden, like *he* always does, and sat at the bar waiting to order a drink. I get *him* a shot of whiskey and a draft beer, probably before most people that were waiting to get a drink. *He* looks at me and without trying on a pick-up line, says to me, "I am going over to a table back there. Come on by when you can take a break." *He* cracks a grin and takes his drinks heading to a booth in the back.

I grab the other bartender and ask to take a 10-minute break as an old friend has entered the bar. The other bartender stares at me sheepishly but then laughs assuming I am going to talk to a man. Well, I was, so the other bartender guessed right. He said it has slowed down anyways and tells me to go on and wishes me good luck.

I pour myself a coke and exit the bar in no time flat. I am always happy to see *him* and I am intrigued to know why *he* has decided to visit me at my workplace. *He* never comes to visit me here. I go over to *him* and sit next to *him* rather than across from *him*. That surprises *him* as much as it surprises me. I feel so happy when *he* is near, I wonder if *he* knows the effect *he* has on me?

"Well, hello stranger!" I say excitedly.

"Hello Tonya!" *He* takes my hand into his. *He* seems to say it happily too and I just love hearing *him* speak my name.

"What brings you by? You know, I think this is the first time you been here. What have you been up too?"

"Well, I have been busy." *He* takes a pull from the draft glass. Continuing on, "I have been busy trying to build the financing for a new business venture."

"This sounds thrilling. Tell me more."

"Well, I thought about opening a bar and I need a bartender to run it."

My poker face is not on tonight as my jaw drops before I figure it out *he* is messin' with me. I tap *him* on the shoulder rather hard.

"Hey, that's no way to treat your potential new business partner!"

My expression changes from glum to surprise all the way to "no shit, you got to be kidding" look on my face.

"I think there is more I need to discuss with you before you sign on."

"Wait a minute," I cry out. "Is this some fancy way to get me to cook you a dinner so you can pitch your proposal?"

"Maybe. Hey, the way I see it, I was thinking whatever you decide, I still get a free meal out of the deal so I don't lose!"

"Then this better be some pitch. What would I have to do?" Now this should trap him, I hope.

He stares at me and without hesitating tells me, "You would have to quit your bartending job and move out West."

My jaw hangs open for a while. I thought, and joking at that, he was gonna tell me I have to invest a hundred dollars and buy some "test products for some MLM scheme." Clearly *he* is serious and wants me to quit the one thing I truly hate doing and take a chance with him to move out West. Wow, is this too good to be true? Where are Maria and Susie when I need to telephone a friend.

"Oh, I know what you are thinking. I am asking a lot and springing it on you at this moment is probably a little unfair. So, tomorrow, I need to come clean on a few things. That way you'll know what I am proposing is sound and honest."

Hmmm, *he* wants to come clean on what? Is *he* a master thief? Oh, and I was getting such a great vibe from *him*. My heart tells me to believe *him* and my mind tells me to believe *him* too. You know what? I believed *him* and I still managed to cook an incredible meal the next night. And *he* talked about a few things and mentioned the business venture. By the end of the night, I cried into *his* arms and we went "out" for a bit in the evening. *He* took me around various places before coming back to my place to seal the deal in the joint venture of us, both personal and in business.

It has been months and I am starting to feel settled in with my new life, new job and new partner, both professionally and personally. I thought I would have been way more resistive about picking up and moving away from what I have built up over the years. To be honest though, what I built up was absolute shit. No, there is no other way to describe it. I had a really, really bad relationship with Mr. Jackass that, well, you know. However, in those dark days, a faint silver lining shown through and now it is bright and shiny happy days.

We moved out to the desert of Las Vegas. Telling that never gets old. I made him take me about the town, both down The Strip and into the Old Town. We covered Las Vegas better than the police ever could in a few short weeks. No offense to the police, thank you for your service, blah blah, I am sure you have heard that a million times.

I am starting to love living out here in Las Vegas. It kinda has a catchy ring to it, don't ya think? But like any tourist town, it has the tourist area, aka, "The Strip" and the rest of the town. We decided to have our office out of a casino because, well, why not. But we live far away from the slot machines and glitzy lights and live life like normal folk. Except we are far from the normal life, so to speak.

I suspect he was somehow different, unlike other guys. Yeah, that was the understatement of the year. *He* confessed some things and, to be honest, I thought about doing a runner. Just leaving and getting away from this creature, beyond human or whatever *he* is. But, I didn't. At first, I was put off, then moved to intrigued, and finally accepted and wanting to understand more. To know the what and why, just like any woman would want to. Except *he* is with me and we swore a blood pact one night. Ok, it might have involved a bottle of vodka in the course of the night but we swore a blood pact and trusted our secrets solemn to one another. In other words, I can't speak of what *he* is until *he* is dead or departed or vanished or I am dead. I really don't know what word to call it for *him*.

I loved it out here and so did *he*. We bought a place right away, cash down no questions ask and it was put in both of our names. Oh yes, I forget to mention this but now I am comfortable talking about it. When we were first getting to know one another, *he* was hesitant about revealing too many things about himself. I was speculating that *he* might have been a master thief or even a drug dealer. I mean, where did all this money come from when it was plainly obvious *he* was not working a job, 9-5 or otherwise. I mean I was working a job as a bartender and it was not a 9-5 job but I was still bringing in money every night. I suppose *he* could have inherited it and was living the dream off of some one's hard work or financial wizardry. I questioned *him* about the 'source of revenue' and *he* was stalling but then revealed the first of many strange things I grew to love about *him*.

He told me about his 'Robin Hood' effect but with a twist. *He* basically robbed from people who stole from others and who would never report the 'robbery' to the police. This list includes but not limited to drug dealers, drug cartels, the mob, rich dishonest bastards, and sports professionals who didn't deserve one dime of their multimillion-dollar bloated contracts. I could not disagree with *his* thinking and never question the ways to which he obtained the funds. Hey, it was there in the various bank accounts legal. Who is going to debate the legality to which the funds were taken? Those people never should have had the money in the first place. Well, that's I how I look at it.

With no money issue worries, it was time to do something good with the money. No, it was not to launder the money *he* gained but more of a better use of us and the funds to do some good. We created an awesome business model and with the financial backing in place, we started to set up shop. It was really exciting especially for me as I found out I could accomplish anything with the right people and right support to help me along the way.

Word quickly spread far and wide and our business venture was more successful than we actually anticipated. It was a dream come true, to be successful, and I was ready to rub it in their faces at the 10-year high school reunion, if I ever bothered to go to those things. The funny thing about this business was we were trying to set something up to keep us busy during the day. However, the clientele was coming in so fast, after 3-4 months, we were looking to expand the business. We had to hire more help and that's when Lisa entered the picture.

One day, *he* mentioned *he* had something to do and will be back in three days. I was fine with it though saddened that I would be on my own. We said our good-bye's and off *he* went, literally. It was one of the strangest things about *him he* warned and I didn't fully appreciate it until *he* was gone. Truth be told, it was frightening when *he* revealed it to me and I, naturally, did not believe what *he* said still demanding proof. I was dead wrong and vow to take people at their word next time.

He told me once *he* has 'special talents' and one was to travel rather quickly. I assume *he* walked fast, not at near hypersonic speed and can transverse the distance between Las Vegas and Salt

Lake City in 20 minutes or less. Of course, it weakens *him* but if I drove that distance I would be tired too. I recall the night *he* proved it to me. Within 18 minutes of leaving our house in Las Vegas, we were in Salt Lake City ordering at a local Greek cuisine chain. Other than being scared senseless, the gyro pita sandwich was rather tasty and their homemade tzatziki sauce is definitely worth mentioning.

He got us back home and we were taking a comp drink at the New York, New York casino bar within the hour. I needed a drink when we were sitting there and asked for and paid for a double of something of higher quality. *He* sat there smiling away and just looking at me with this big ole grin. I thought about it long and hard, well, between the first drink finished and the second drink arriving soon thereafter. I was unhappy with my life before *he* comes along and saves it. So *he* has a few issues and unhuman talents, but we benefit from it all so why am I complaining? I leaned over and to kiss *him* saying, "OK, I surrender. I am yours. You win!"

Of course, *he* hits a royal flush at that very moment at the bar electronic dealer. *He* pauses to look at the screen and then back to me. Which was a better decision on *his* part, by the way, to stare at me longer than a computer screen. I remember what *he* said.

"Tonya, because of you, I am comfortable. You are the only one." *He* kisses me and then waves the bartender for another comp drink and cashes out on *his* winnings. Not that we need the money anymore but it is still fun to take as much money as we can from any casino.

What more could a girl want. I had it all, both at the casino that very moment and living with *him* in the desert. My life was so much better and I felt I have achieved success in life. Cheers to me!

I was sitting at the front desk at our office not knowing what to expect that day. I was hoping it would be a prospective person that just bombs the interview. Maybe spills coffee on themselves, dresses inappropriately accompanied with foul perfume, or just basically screws it up. It was none of above as Lisa showed up ... positive, full of energy and ready to rock the interview. In a way, I was sad that what we had between us was now shared with another person, and a pretty, younger woman at that. Still, I trusted *him* and we endured through the "Enthralling Days of Lisa." What was even stranger, I'd really like Lisa even if I was jealous of her at first. But her fate was sealed, it was a matter of time before she expired.

After the interview and all the usual stuff, Lisa began her employment with us. It can also be said that Lisa was now the third point of the triangle in our little group which used to consist of only *him* and I. Oh, how the times have changed. At first, we did not know how adding an additional person was going to affect the work relationship between us. But, Lisa adjusted rather quickly to our unusual style and we loved her from the start.

We always had a laid-back work culture. So, incorporating the "after shift relaxation and have a drink on the sofa over-looking The Strip" was a hit as the three of us formed a great working team. It was no surprise that after a few months, Lisa felt a calling to a something different, something more. She had the travel bug and wanted to travel like *him* and I always did. Except, she had it bad and it concerned *him* to the point he knew something I didn't.

And it was not revealed until after the fact. Lisa was going to die if she traveled to Europe.

In the end, Lisa did travel to Europe and she did die. We knew what was going to happen and I blamed *him* for not stopping it. He had no answer as though he knew all along that Lisa was going to die at some point, whether in Europe, North America or otherwise and he could not stop it from happening. I remember vividly the night it happened as I witnessed him reacting to it before the news of it became official. I gazed into his eyes and and only saw blackness, emptiness. I have never seen him like he was that night. I cried both for Lisa and for *him* because her death affected *him* more than I first realized.

I still blamed him and it caused a huge rift in our special relationship. I finally made the decision to leave and go visit my parents and he decided to venture off to New Orleans. I feel that after my attempted suicide, this was the second worst decision in my life. Impulsively, I was mad at him and wanted a break from him. I now realize he knew all along that he was never going to see me again. I wish now I would have said a proper good-bye to *him*. I royally messed up and can never make up for it, but rather only try to make amends for my clouded decisions back then. I am so sorry, dear. I messed up again and I pray I don't do it a third time.

It was days later that I first hear of the news. I feel like I should have died at the exact moment but apparently, I am still around for another reason. Mind you, it is still painful to be reminded so excuse me if I stop for no reason. My feelings for *him* seem to be much stronger now that *he* is gone versus when *he* was standing next to me. I don't know why either. Here is the recap from the news on the events that were recorded from someone standing nearby.

I remember reading from the eyewitness account in the USA TODAY newspaper a day later:

.... I was walking along the river at night and there were a fair number of people out and about. However, there was one particular group of three people that I remember vividly.

I see this fairly pretty, yet older woman in a long black cloak that was odd even for New Orleans. Next to her was male who reminded me of Lurch from the Adams Family TV show. I mean this dude looked like he won Mortician of the Year award multiple years running. Ok, I thought, what is this old, dead-looking dude doing with a woman dressed like she is the guest speaker at the Witches Convention?

I hung back, fearing for my life, but was intrigued especially why this other man, who appeared normal, was with these two crazy individuals. I figure something is going down I should be recording this. I have seen some hustles in this town but this other man is about to be taken for everything he owns.

The female starts to sit next to him and the other guy is standing looking about, like he is watching for the police or somebody. Luckily, none of them see me or are not concerned and see me as non-threatening. The female moves away from the 'mark' and stands in front of him like she is about to do some weird lap dance.

Well, she does some crazy dance, gyrating in all sorta weird directions and then claps her hands together. The 'mark' shakes like he is feeling pain and then the Lurch dude shoots him twice

65

causing the dude to fall over. The woman and Lurch simply pat the dude's head and walk away. I called the Police right away, both for the male shot dead and for my own safety. I am tellin' ya, it was some crazy (word omitted).

The papers and media seemed to have a field day with *his* murder. They called it The Sacrifice and reported a rogue witches' coven claimed responsibility right away. It was later retracted. They called in local Voodoo Experts to give their take and even a medium rattled off she felt the devil was present in New Orleans over the last week during the time of *his* murder. It got so ludicrous that no one took it serious. Well, almost no one because they identified the body and contacted me four days later. My name and phone was in *his* wallet as the "In Case of Emergency" contact. Also, a lawyer representing *him* called me two weeks later.

First, the police called me to notify me of *his* death and questioned me to see if I knew anything or knew anyone was after *him*. I told the Police I am coming down to New Orleans and met with the detective in charge of the case. This guy seems like he grew up in New Orleans all his life and spoke with a local accent to attest to it. It took me awhile to fully understand him and, at best, I caught every third word of what came out of his mouth. Still, I give him credit as he tried and went by the book questioning everyone and suspicious of me and even the guy who gave the firsthand account.

I was finally exonerated after Day 3 of the police interviews and it was confirmed in the papers. At first, I was the estranged shady business partner from Las Vegas who had a reason to take him out. I was glad the retraction was published a week later at the bottom of page 16 of section B. Still, my name was cleared and eventually the investigation had no other leads. Even the video from the phone proved worthless as it dark and blurry, barely making anything or anyone visible. Maybe it was tampered with or maybe the killer blurred it that way. We will never know the truth.

I eventually met up with the witness and we had coffee and beignets one morning at Café Du Monde. It felt strange and I watched the video from his phone, the same phone that recorded it firsthand of *his* death. I dropped the phone at the moment and have never watched the video footage again until 6 months later for a different reason to do so.

After that, I never saw the witness again. We didn't become Facebook friends and did not exchange email addresses. There was no reason to be in contact with him ever although I did appreciate him actually meeting me and for doing what he did. I haven't heard of him dying mysteriously or suspiciously so there blows my conspiracy theory. *His* death was ruled a homicide under suspicious circumstances along with weird ritualistic movements but they never charged anyone for *his* death and no other witches coven claimed responsibility. Even the Satanist were quiet on this one, shrugging their shoulders, thinking it was even weird for them.

Second, the law office contacted me soon after I was cleared of all suspicions. Funny how their phone call was perfectly timed to my police affair concluding but I guess they all work together, don't they? Anyways, I received the phone call and was instructed to meet with the lawyers for the disposition of *his* estate. I was figuring that the business would become solely mine and that was that. Boy, was I wrong and the surprise on my face was rather, well, somebody should have taken a photo because I was utterly beyond shocked.

I decided I was done with New Orleans, both clearing up any police investigation and having one last chicken e'touffee in the French Quarter. I had a flight to the Law Office in, of all places, Detroit. Well, maybe I can catch a hockey game if the local hockey team is in town on a home game. *He* did mention about a Greek section of downtown Detroit, maybe I can see what *he* was always raving about.

After devouring a delicious gyro sandwich in one of the restaurants in Greektown, downtown Detroit, I made my way to the Law Office of some ritzy Detroit law firm. There, the story of my life takes another turn for the better.

I would visit the Law Office expecting to sign some forms to get full and sole control of the business. Easy enough. Instead, I got more, a lot more.

I arrive at the law firm. Ironically, there is a brunette at the reception desk, the very same desk I use to sit at in our office, and she politely asks for my details and such. I supply them to her and her expression changes immediately to almost flirty and smiling at me a lot. I thought it was odd or maybe she is just overly friendly to female clients. Either way, I sit down to patiently wait in the lobby but two lawyers spring out their offices in less than 45 seconds. Well, give this place props for their excellent and efficient customer service.

I always knew there were secrets *he* still held back from me after all those moments we shared. I knew some of *his* secrets and would never tell a soul on what *he* could do but it seems that even *he* kept a lot of things from me. Until now.

"Ms. Tonya. We are pleased you are here for the will reading. We express our condolences on your loss. We understand he meant the world to you as you meant the world to him. We also would like to take this opportunity to offer our services at a reasonable rate should you, ah, require legal representation in the foreseeable future. Consider us first, Ms. Tonya. You won't be disappointed as we are experts in these type of matters." The lawyer flashes a cheesy smile after his sales pitch that was a little too creepy for me.

It was though they knew something I did not. Maybe they should just get to the reading of the will. At that moment, I realize I am the only one here for the reading so it suggests everything is going to me. It was kinda sad for a moment to think about as *he* never did mention parents, siblings, or friends. However, it does not matter anymore, does it? I nod my head as the lead lawyer is patiently waiting for me to give the go ahead.

"To my one and only Tonya. You were the world to me and everything. I leave you the business we so built from scratch. Mind you, go visit the office sometime soon as there is a letter on the table waiting to be opened and read by only you."

The lawyer pauses for a moment as I sigh. He gets me a glass of water and I drink it all. He smiles back at me and tells me, "But wait there is a lot more."

I shake my head in disbelieve. More, he says?

"Tonya. I want you to be set in this life. I bequeath to you all my properties, possessions, and financial accounts. I trust the law office will make the transition to you less painful and all fees and taxes have been pre-paid. Live a great life and move on, get past me but never forget me. Love you always and don't ever forget the great times in Vegas."

I am short of breath. "So, what are these properties he mentioned?"

The lawyer gazes at me. "Would you like a drink first?"

Why is he stalling? "Sure. But tell me. Now."

He calls the receptionist who promptly opens a bottle of champagne to pour me a drink. I take a drink and feel the calming effect yet I am so anxious to hear what the lawyer is about to recite to me.

"Ms. Tonya. You now have a property here in Detroit."

Ok, I suppose this has some benefits. Maybe I can check out what this city has to offer. There is the Motown Studios and some Casinos downtown. Maybe I can rent it out on Airbnb or something.

The lawyer continues on. "Sorry. You also have properties and homes in the following locations."

Did he say following? As in plural?

"As I was saying, in addition to the property here in the Motor City, you also have properties in the following cities: New Orleans, Louisiana; Albuquerque, New Mexico; Salt Lake City, Utah; and Nassau, Bahamas."

"Holy Shit." I could not hold it back at all and really didn't care to remain lady-like at a moment like this. The lawyer pauses for a moment and continues on.

"Ms. Tonya. In addition to *his* properties which are now yours. Mind you they are all paid for and escrow accounts set-up to take care of taxes and utilities, you are also the sole owner of all *his* possessions in each of the properties in addition to all *his* personal effects. Also, the bank accounts and their contents are now yours."

"Bank accounts? How many and how much?"

The lawyer lets out a laugh and then regains his composure. "Ah yes, the bank accounts. We have six of them listed and the amount totals in excess of......"

I was waiting for a drum roll.

"Yes, how much?" I anxiously ask.

"Yes. In excess of $15 million dollars. Congratulations. You are a millionaire many times over Ms. Tonya. Just sign the forms and it is all yours. As he said, our fee has been taken care of." The lawyer smiles like he just became a millionaire himself from this client fees' too.

My heart is beating so fast and nearly thumping out of my chest. I think of the houses around the country and one overseas. The ones *he* originally planned to share with me but never did. I think about the money that he and I were going to live out our lives together until we were old that we will never be able to do. But most of all, as I am signing the forms, is I need to get to the office and read the letter he left for me and only me on the table.

The lawyer makes one last sales pitch, "If you need representation, our law firm will most happy to represent you."

They, the lawyers, will always advertise themselves to the bitter end.

After the initial shock of the payout from the inheritance, I was both in a state of awe and a state of confusion. I mean, it is not every day that someone receives over $15 million in cash plus houses all over North America. I guess I really have done well for myself and this is from a girl who never attended college. However, there is the one thing that keeps pinging my mind and heart. The one little line about the letter waiting for me in the office in Las Vegas.

I assumed that neither one of us had visited the office since we closed up shop weeks ago. It seems that was not the case and I need to get my millionaire rich ass out there. For once in my life, I look forward with anticipation as to what the unread letter may say. I always knew *he* kept something back, but I never imagined the payday *he* gave me today. Perhaps the letter might shed some facts and give me the closure. Probably not, but at least I get to go home and get ready to sort out and chart out my life from this moment forward. I book the next flight to Las Vegas, First Class naturally.

I land at McCarren Airport and take an over-priced limo ride to our office at the casino. It does not matter as I have millions at my disposal and might as well start spending some of that dinero on everything and anything. Honestly, what is the point holding back now? Nothing but the best, after all, that is what *he* always wanted for me, wasn't it?

I walk those last few steps toward the office on the third floor. Retrieving the keys from the casino manager, he had the nerve to offer to have a drink with him despite me telling him of my partner's demise. The nerve of some guys. I get the keys and take the elevator exiting on the third floor. I step slowly towards our office, towards what we use to share that now seems so long ago. I enter the office and get flooded with the memories of a time so far distant in the past. I see the table and two items sitting on the top. I walk precariously toward the table trying not to think of *him* nor of Lisa though I find it difficult to do so.

I stop a few feet from the table as I immediately recognize one of the items on the table once it comes into focus. I succumb to tears in my eyes as I see before me a box that can only be described as containing a ring inside. I wipe the tears from both of my eyes and walk forward only stopping in front of the table. Looking out toward The Strip like *he* always enjoyed, I look out and then stare straight down to the table in front of me. I see the envelope yet reach for the box. I instinctively reach for the ring box and open it to my utter astonishment. What I behold is the most beautiful yet precious engagement ring I have ever had the pleasure to lay my eyes upon. The diamonds sparkle like the stars of the night. I automatically put on the ring and it fits like a glove, like it was always meant for me to wear.

I, of course, burst into tears upon putting the engagement ring on my finger. Then, the full realization of what was to happen. Oh, *he* was going to propose to me and I never saw it coming. I will never know how *he* was going to do it, how *he* was going to phrase it, and how I was going to react to it. I fall down to my knees in a fit of emotional state and scream out *his* name sobbing mercilessly until I could not cry anymore. These were those moments in life that one never gets a second chance. Tears flow unchecked like a river from my eyes.

I recover eventually and reach over for the envelope after donning my newly acquired engagement ring on my left hand. It was the least I could do. I accept it as I shout it out loudly the affirmation, only praying *he* heard my resounding acceptance, somehow. I reach over for the sealed letter still sitting on the table. I open it at once and read it out loud.

Dearest Tonya,

When one sums up the value of their life, one can't always predict the people who we come across accidentally who renew our faith in life.

I started to cry right away because I at this moment, I understand the true love we had for each other. I look down to my ring and see the diamond sparkle back at me. I read on.

I had tremendous power but knew my time was limited. What I did with it and what I could have done can be debated among the those who survive and remember me. I have altered many lives but none stand out more than yours, my one true love. I cannot fathom the pain you felt to be in such a position but I can stand testament as a benefactor of you, both alive and as a part of your life. I will forever remember the knowledge of you and your, yes your, impact on my own life. I only wish I would have presented this ring as a token of my love for you sooner. I often wonder what your answer would be.

Love you forever and beyond

PS – They may be after you because of me. Take the money and the safe houses and use them well. There is a way to defeat the two of them. My only regret is not figuring it out in time. You will have to find others to help you along the way. I know this sounds clear as grey but heed my words, Tonya.

I sat there for a long time. I know at some point I refilled my drink but it just sat there on the table, untouched. Instead, I was holding the letter, gazing at the beautiful ring, and looking out the window and onto The Strip, like *he* always did but will never do. I cannot recall the time but realize it was the dawn of a new day when the sun rose from the East and shown onto me. I clutched the letter tightly before folding it and stuffing it in my pocket. I get up, walk out, lock the door and, in my mindset, set myself on what needs to be done as the ring sparkles the reflection upwards into my line of sight.

Ok. First, I needed a vacation. Get out of dodge and clear my head. I guess it was time to go check out the property in Nassau Bahamas. Why not? I needed to relax, rethink and reorganize my life. Why should I do it in a AC office when I can do it with the sea breeze blowing on my face while Julio the barkeep brings me a tropical drink.

Back in Detroit, I did decide to retain the law firm as my legal representation and appoint them to handle my estate. I know, I know. Never trust a lawyer but *he* paid them enough so I figure they would be sympathetic to me. At the very least, they know the estate better than anyone else, especially me. They would take care of the deed transfers and establish the holdings into my name, for a modest fee of course. Well, there went 25K of my inheritance, but at least I won't have to worry about such matters any more. It didn't matter arguing what fees were prepaid or not. I am sure they come up with some scheme to get my money, one way or another. I should be happy, since I am paying them on my own accord.

He really thought of everything. Each of the properties has the necessary things itemized and a trustworthy person maintaining the said property. Their caretaker services were even prepaid for a year. Wow, this was too easy. I guess this is the moment I should be shedding another tear for *him*. Hell, I cry every day for *him* but the show must go on and I have to be in right frame of mind, at least until I track down his killers. Even if it costs me my own life which is more likely the case. Maybe I should update my will then. I wonder how much the law firm will charge me this time?

I am getting used to First Class seating as it makes air travel so much easier now and fun to do. They are much friendlier, the amenities are there, the food is better, and seat is ever so comfy. I am so envious of *his* mode of transportation but truth be told, I did kinda hate it. Oh sure, it speeds up the travel time but I always felt like I was going to throw up and was so nauseous for an hour afterwards. I much prefer the airplane method especially since I am racking up those all-important Delta Skymiles. I should be pretty close to a free ticket to Hawaii by now.

Oh yes, being one of the first ones off the plane also means you don't have to wait as long in the immigration and customs line. Those can be such a waste of time. I have better things to be doing. Like looking for the sign with my name on it for the limo to pick me up and take me to my beach front house outside of Nassau. See how much quicker things are moving now?

The driver takes me to my humble beach hut in Nassau: the gated property with 4,000-sq. ft. of awesomeness. It is times like this that

I really miss *him* and think about what if, could if, whatever if, but it didn't for whatever reason. I did promise to toast the first drink in *his* honor. OMG, look at the that pool and the view to the sea or ocean, oh, I am so going to love this place. I may end up moving and living here permanently.

So maybe Julio the barkeep did not bring my tropical fruity drink to my beach side table. Actually, her name was Rosalina and she was quite good at being there when I needed her and disappearing when I wanted to be alone. I never asked what deal or arrangement she might have had with *him* and I will never want to know. She did have her own place on the property separate from the main house. And she makes an incredible breakfast spread. I trust her, at least, for feeding me breakfast and sometimes cooking dinner too.

Yet, after the 7th day, I was starting to get island fever and felt the need to return to my adobe in the Nevada desert. I make the travel arrangement and inform Rosalina I will be leaving. I start to envision her throwing wild parties every night I am not here but as long as she cleans it up and no one goes in or uses my bedroom, yeah, I'd rather not think about what happens when I am not here. You got a good thing going Rosalina, don't screw it up. I will be back in two months, make sure the pool is cleaned and fresh sheets are on the bed.

On the return flight to our, I mean, my home in Las Vegas, I re-read of my plans to move forward and my strategy for my new life. One, I should visit all the properties in the other cities so I can, I don't know, potentially live there and maybe search for any clues *he* might have left behind. Though this may not be a good plan as I found zilch in Nassau other than a great cook and that the sea breeze blows nicely in the open-air house at night. Ah, that was nice to sleep like that and the privacy gate made me feel even more secure. Two, I truly want to hunt down *his* killers. Except, I all I have to go on is an older-looking dude and woman in a black cloak.

Good plan. Maybe I should try to accomplish part one first before tackling part two. You never know, something might just fall into my lap. Oh, the plane has landed at McCarren. I debark from the plane as it is time to go find my driver so he can collect my luggage and I can go home. I think the next city to visit should be Albuquerque. Why, may you ask why I selected this one? Well, for starters, I have never been there.

About a week later, I arrived at Sunport International Airport in Albuquerque and was completely taken in by the sheer beauty, not to mention the altitude, of this city in the heart of New Mexico. There was something magical about the West that initially drew me out when *he* first asked me to accompany *him* to Las Vegas. Now, I love the West and the pure tranquility and expansiveness with some mountain range in the distance. To me, this is paradise. Though sitting on the beach a few weeks back was also paradise, just a different paradise saturated with fruity cocktails and salty ocean breezes. There is a lot less humidity here in the West though, but still enough sunshine.

I was picked up at the airport by the limo service as I am starting to get used to this ritual and I am not complaining at all. The driver was a local guy and he knew when to keep quiet. It is different from taxis drivers who seem to think they will get a bigger tip the more they talk. This driver was professional all the way but I had to ask him where he would go eat if he was impressing a date. He directed me in the northeast area of the city and that ended his part of the conversation until we arrived at yet another Tonya awesome residence.

This house was set in the traditional Southwest style and no expense was spared. I have to admit, I was beginning to wonder what I may uncover about *him* or should I count my blessings and call it a day?

I pre-arranged for the caretaker to meet me here once my plane landed. True to his word, he was standing present on the porch waiting for the limo to arrive. He greeted me with respect and grace though it seems as though he was coached on what to say to the next 'owner.' It bothered me for a bit but he was well-paid and was happy to give me the tour of the house and all the amenities that come with it. Including the hardly ever used, practically brand-new Jeep parked in the two-car garage. I guess I don't have to call upon Uber now to go cruise downtown.

Once the house tour was complete – I even got a water bottle along the way – he asked me to sign a few forms to complete the transfer of ownership including for the Jeep. He hinted about how he was on the payroll for another 10 months should his services be required afterwards. I guess if I had a good gig like this one, I would want to ensure its longevity too.

I spent the next few days clearing my head and just living life. Something I haven't done for a long time. I did not consider slinging warm bottles of beers to drunken patrons as living life. But that was another life and certainly my future is much brighter these days. I had a crazy thought to drive out in the desert and reach higher enlightenment but I would have to score some weed or LSD. Maybe if I played some Pink Floyd or The Doors and drank some bourbon, do you think that would that do the trick? Or is the trip achievable without mind-altering drugs and only by acceptance of self-consciousness? Maybe I shouldn't drive into the desert on anything after all.

After a few days, I went to a fancier restaurant in the NW side of town. The air was dry in the evening but I have been starting to get use to the climate and altitude of the beautiful city. I went along with the recommendation of my housekeeper as a decent place to eat and maybe over indulged a wee bit there. I opted to walk it off as there was public park nearby. Besides, I need to kill some time after the second glass of a decent local bubbly wine before I get behind the wheel.

I thought the park would be calm and peaceful but that was exactly the opposite of what I received. Rather than a leisurely stroll along the trail enjoying the evening, alone and noise-reduced, I came upon a most troubling series of events.

I could hear a couple shouting at one another even before I seen them arguing with my own eyes. There was an older gent, nicely dressed, screaming obscenities to a young, more vibrant female in a loose-fitting black evening dress. She had brilliant red hair, cut short but was larger than life in returning the volley of shouts to the taller older man. Then, out of nowhere, the taller gentleman, well not a gentleman anymore, cold-cocked the female right in the face. I swear I could hear the punch, bone on bone. She fell backwards and wailed out as she fell back to the ground.

That's when I starting screaming to top of my lungs. I could see the male winding up for another attack but realizing he had a witness, volleyed some obscenity to me before fleeing the scene. I wanted to chase him down and give him in return what he just dished out, but my belly was still full from the meal earlier.

Instead, I ran over to the woman who was rather distressed. She was shouting this and that, incoherence phrases and such. I bent down to feebly attempt to calm her down as she was initially trembling in fear. I eventually soothe her and she then relaxes a bit, more for the safe protection I am currently providing. I am still vigilant in case the coward of a man returns and takes vengeance on me as well. The smell of wine permeating from her suggests the classic alcohol-fueled domestic argument. Still, her face did not need to be used as target practice and I begin to phone the police. She reacts quickly anticipating what I was about to do, reporting the assault to the police, and takes my phone out of my hand.

"No police." She breathes heavily. "Don't ask. Just no police. Please do as I ask of you."

I am in a quandary as what to do. However, she starts to speak before I had time to think about deciding my next course of action despite her pleads. She stands up and I follow suit. She tells me she needs to phone for a taxi but I offer to give her a lift to her house or a safer place to stay. She thanks me in kind and we walk to my vehicle. I feel confident about thwarting something that could have ended much worse.

I try to make small talk but she is only staring out the window, lost with a face of hopelessness. Desperation. I attempt to change the mood and mention I only just arrived here and do not know my way around town. She guides us toward her house and she starts to liven up a bit, perhaps because of thinking of the present and not what her future lies await. I repeatedly ask her if she is going to be safe at the house we are driving to. She waves it off mentioning it is her house, not his. She was more confident by the time we arrive at her house versus leaving the park 40 minutes ago.

We pull up to house, eventually. Boy, talk about living out in the sticks. Or what is the term here, living out in the desert? I think she owns the last house in the city before it is desert and the vastness of empty desert land. We cross a cattle guard and proceed up the driveway. I stop the vehicle and put it in park. I take her hand, silently, though I want to tell her I would be ready to be a witness if she decides to phone the police. But my suspicions are correct, this is type of woman that will not be contacting the police.

In a surprise move, she leans over to me. She then gives me a hug as I slowly return the gesture despite the logistical gear box in a SUV. She then whispers something in my ear but I could not make it out. However, I feel a sense of euphoric giddiness. I let go but smile back at her. She offers to cook dinner for me as a gesture of thanks. Two woman out in the desert and maybe a bottle of wine as she phrases it. I, for whatever reason, say yes not really thinking about but just answering the question posed to me. She stares back at me intensively, as studying me, and breaks the contact only to grab my phone from the console to input her address in my contacts list. Rather brass gesture but I don't feel threatened by her at all. She just makes me happy and smiley. I wave good-bye to her and drive off crossing the cattle guard before realizing what time it was. I really need to figure out where my house is again.

Have I been so wrapped up in the recent events that I cannot relax? Yes, I want to find *his* killers so bad but have not formulated a good plan or even a place to start. It is not like one can send a signal to all the Immortals running, flying or floating around and ask them to give me a call. I don't even know how they operate or even if they care that one of their own was killed.

I still cannot get the concept of the fact to be immortal until one is no long immortal. Isn't that the whole idea of being immortal, that you don't die? Then why did *he* die or more importantly, what is powerful enough to kill an immortal? Yes, perhaps I should take a break from all of this and go have dinner with a normal person who just been through a traumatic event. Maybe I should stop for a bit and interact with normal human folk. Wouldn't it be funny if she is one of them, the very one I have been trying to seek out? I hope, at the very least, that her cooking is decent. I am not bringing an Italian red this time as I had bad luck with that choice in the past. Definitely a red blend, something easier to drink this time.

I got ready for my 'date.' I thought about it all day and I compared it to the list of people I talk with or consider a friend over the last 12 months. After a depressing revelation in that two of the people are dead, I opted for the choice of free food from this unique stranger. After all, it is not an issue anymore and good conversation in a strange town with a complete stranger. I could have done much worse meeting somebody at a nightclub.

As I drive to her Southwest villa, I am overcome with emotions both good and bad. I am anxious for meeting and interacting with someone new, it is almost like a date. Yet, I feel overwhelmed with guilt for not progressing forward in my defiant act of revenge. I stare down at the engagement ring decorating my left hand as I now wear it all the time. Both for the love and a reminder.

I get out of the Jeep and slowly take my time gazing at the surroundings. I love the the sunset here out West. It is so picturesque with the desert in the foreground and an incredible Mesa in the background. I feel like I have been transported to an old film set of a spaghetti Western. Instead of armed with a six-shooter, I'm carrying a lovely Argentinian red blend. I draw it upon seeing her waiting for me at the door. She smiles in kind and invites me in her humble adobe.

The house was decorated in a wide array of period pieces and different regions of the world. I thought it was rather odd but I suppose it would make sense after a glass or two of red wine. Besides, the aromas of dinner permeate the living room as we progress to the dining area and I was more concerned on when we start feasting.

After a wonderful and delicious meal, I am so sated yet I yearn for something sweet. Perhaps I should have brought a chocolate torte or something but it's too late and she doesn't look like a person who eats a lot of desserts. She asks me to refill our glasses and to move to the spacious living room where she will accompany me after tiding up. That was a deal I was happy to sign off on as I hate washing the dishes. I move to the living room to await her presence. It gives me time to stare in wonder at some of the arts pieces.

Now things start to feel funny. No, it was not the food. That was so yummy. And no, it was not the alcohol. It was something else. I could not describe it but I feel I was about to find out one way or another before the night was out. I start to slowly sip the wine of the second glass rather than guzzling as I did with the first glass. I remove my shoes and reside on the sofa, rather cozy the sofa is I might add, and wait for her to join me. God only knows what will happen next. Maybe she is the Immortal I am seeking and will reveal herself in due time. Or maybe she will reveal herself and her feelings toward me. Hmmm, maybe I have had a little too much wine to drink, thus, it will induce the decision easier to make. Either way, something is about to be revealed.

She enters the living room already having removed her shoes. Apparently, it must be a woman thing or just the idea of being more comfortable in bare feet. She glides over to the other love seat picking up her glass of wine in the process before soothing to her resting spot. I start to feel more uncomfortable but I resign the feelings inside not giving away any emotion or sign of distress. She only looks at me keenly, never blinking for a minute. Like how a predator stares at its prey.

She takes a drink from the wine goblet before telling a monologue of a funny story years ago when she moved here from the Eastern seaboard. Her details were so vivid I almost feel like I was lifted and actually walking along Coney Island. I blink for a second and she gets to the funny part and we all laugh and joke. Maybe my paranoia got the best of me. Or not.

I am still chuckling away and almost snorted the wine back thru my nose. I put the wine glass down and, as raising my head, I see him. No not *him*. Rather, I see an older man walking from a back room and entering the living room. I start to scream but for the second time in my life, no sound comes out or it is not very loud. The male only checks me out once before residing next to the woman. Come to think of it, I never did catch her name.

"Hello my darling Sid. It is nice of you to join us." The woman replies.

"Anything for you, my beautiful Fiona." The older man quickly says.

Well, at least, I now know their names.

They both laugh out loud in a menacing cackle. The kind that gives you the chills up and down the arms. As I knew because I have the chills from being frightened out of my wits at this very moment. I am still in shock on what is exactly happening and my brain refuses to process it. The last vivid memory of my old self on this particular night was Fiona and Sid standing up and slowly walking toward me and those fateful words she uttered before it happened, the transformation.

Fiona yells out, "It's time!" And then it started to happen as I start to scream in the most loud and audible sort of way. It was already too late though.

There was a fleeing moment when I thought I was dreaming all this. Maybe Fiona slipped me a mickey or I drank too much and passed-out. It could have been just a dream. It should appropriately be labeled a nightmare but that's beside the point. It does not matter anymore as I was very alive, kicking and screaming, when the male, Sid, grabbed me to restrain me.

Fiona then came at me with those blackened eyes and I was beyond screaming at this point. My lungs and throat were already too sore from the previous wails earlier. I am surprised I didn't pass out as one can only take in so much stress and terror. The body would act defensively and shut down, protecting itself from any further damage. I was thinking maybe I am getting immune to this type of stress after the episode with *him* and the bathroom incident many months ago. My brain switches to focus on auditory sounds and I only then realize Fiona and Sid are chanting something in a foreign language. I could not tell nor guess what language it could be. It may have been Klingon for all I knew.

With Sid having a death grip on me, there was no escape. Fiona is still blathering away in her own manner. For whatever strange reason, earlier I was glad I ate something but now I could feel that maybe it wasn't such a good thing. The food is fighting a fierce battle in my lower abdomen which is causing me physical pain not to mention the chanting is giving me a headache.

Then I start to laugh at the inappropriate moment. Compare it to the kind of inappropriate laughing at a drama performance, classical recital, or at a funeral. At first, I was going to ask how long is this chant going to go on because I need to sit down soon. Then, I thought about what music I could add to Fiona's chant to give it some flavor. Perhaps, some drums too? Something like dah dah da dah dah da.... you get the idea?

I think my outburst of laughter might have pissed her off or I interrupted the important part. The ending is all I can only hope. To be honest, it all sounded the same after a while to me anyways. Fiona stares at me directly, like she is going to punish me or kill me. I figure I am going to die tonight so punishing me does not have a lot of meat to it. I guess she could slap me around a little before killing me or sacrificing me. I think if they do carve me up or eat my heart, I hope it causes them a stomach ache. Uh oh, something has changed. Here it comes.

Fiona stops chanting. Thank goodness for that and at least one of my prayers has been answered. Fiona takes her hands and puts them together with the palms together. She then raises them above her head and splits them to the sides arcing them to in front of her and thrusts them forward toward me, striking me in the chest. The pure shock wave and force was unlike anything I have ever felt. Sid is still holding me tightly as I collapse to the ground.

The next part can be described as either what might have happened, what I have dreamed, or what happens when one drinks too much red wine at dinner. Whichever one it is or a combination of all three, it can best be described as dream-like state yet I am fully conscious. Yes, it is not supposed to make sense because one is not ever supposed to experience this beyond a physical or a spiritual state. Not even when one smokes weed either but I am betting that might be the closest way to defining it. I have never inhaled for the record.

I was laying there on the ground. Sid takes one of my hands and Fiona takes the other one. Together we raise and I don't just mean I stand up on my legs. I mean we raise, up and up through the roof and ascending high above the ground quickly until we pass the clouds and some birds along the way. No, it was not a flock of seagulls though that would have been hysterical. Then I should be running, not flying, so far away.

The eerie thing about this, not that floating high above the Earth wasn't eerie enough, was there was absolutely no sound. Nada. Nothing. Zilch. Not even a squawk from the birds that flew right pass us. It was though I was deaf or I am coming to grips with the fact that I might be dead. At least I am going up and not down, that was a comforting thought.

Maybe I spoke, I mean thought, too soon as we stop. They both let go of my hands yet I still remained in stasis amongst the clouds. They floated in front of me and each putting a hand forward, thrusted once again upon my chest. I flew backwards at top speed back toward the Earth. My body, or soul, was swarmed with a tingling sensation that was beyond controllable. It was a drunken buzz, a runners' high and an acid trip all rolled into one. It felt as if every emotion decided to play - from pain and sensual all the way to ending at euphoria with a host of others in between being experienced all at the same time. My mind was flooded and overloaded with thoughts racing, memories flashing, and ideas bursting to the scene. I remember seeing the world spin about at crazy speeds and as I approached the ground, I knew it was this instant I was going to die. Yet, I somehow felt at peace. It must have been the adrenalin kicking in. The ground is nearly there and I braced for impact. It was at this very moment, I blacked out.

I was awakened by birds singing outside my window. I wonder if it was the same birds from the other night? For once, it did not bother me. Sing away, my feathered friends as tomorrow I am getting a cat. I felt a little sore and slowly jumped out of bed to go use the bathroom. I discovered the awful, putrid smell that hit me after a second or two. It smelled as if something was decaying in the bathroom or is it in the bedroom. I wonder if there is a dead animal in the vents? I enter the bathroom and lift the toilet seat and noticed in a flash the mold that has grown in the toilet bowl.

I almost throw up. Luckily for me though, the best time to throw up is when one is looking down toward a toilet bowl. I reach for and hit the flush handle hoping the mold and the awful smell flushes down the drain. I suddenly realize in an instant the horrible smell is emanating from me. It is definitely time to change brands of deodorant. I raise my head slowly toward the mirror and jump back at the horror I see staring back at me. It is though I have slept for many days straight. I appear somewhat different and hope a shower will help the cause out.

I go out the living room and it smells funny too. It was as though nothing had been disturbed for a period of time. I begin to wonder how long was I out? More importantly, how did I get back to the house? Panic starts to overtake me and I sit down on a chair at the kitchen table. I see my phone laying there along with my keys, purse and other items. They are all perfectly placed in the table. Now I know something is not right as I never place items is such perfect alignment. Who does that anyways, surely nobody I know.

I grab the phone and see the main screen coming in clear. I have a dozen missed calls and 100+ Facebook notices. It is also worth mentioning, six days have passed since I went to Fiona's for dinner. Six Days! What the hell has happened? What have I been doing for six days? Surely, I could not have slept the entire time, nobody does that except Rip Van Winkle. Why am not hungry, thirsty or have a really strong urge to go to the bathroom? Wait a minute on the last one, that might be a part of the strong putrid odor in the bedroom. But the hunger and thirst, now that is bizarre, is it not?

I moved over to the sofa and laid there for a long time, thinking about the events of a week ago from the dinner party night. I closed my eyes and relived every moment until I blacked out before hitting the ground. After a while, I had the plan put together and knew what I must do. I decided I have to do a lot of things but some take priority over others. So, one, hired a cleaning staff to clean my house. Two, take a bath to wash away the filth. Three, figure out what it means to be an Immortal now.

Yup, I said it. I hope you were paying attention. I am an Immortal. Live forever and all what comes with it. Well, let me rephrase it. Live forever until I die. Yes, I think that is the proper was to say it these days. It is a little more correct or at least it was for *him*.

So yes. I am immortal. Fiona and Sid must have the power to create us and obviously take it away too. Now that I am immortal, should I wear a silly costume? Perhaps a velvet cloak and appear like a vampire? Or maybe something sexy like a toga to give it a Greek goddess look? Maybe something simple as wearing all black because, well, I really don't know but its seems to fit.

Who would have figured I would get the 'power', certainly *he* didn't or was all of this some sort of a master plan? I want to go seek out Fiona but when I returned to her house later in the week, it was already packed away for the season. I must seek her out as she is the only one who can tell me what I am supposed to do. There was no manual left on the kitchen table, no email or a text and I can't YouTube it. I did check Google to put my mind to ease but it eventually led me to a Rick Astley video. Go figure. Wait a minute, is he one of us?

I guess I have to figure it out all on my own. I'm not going shoot myself to prove it. I did try cutting my arm many months ago. Ironic that me cutting myself way back when is what led me to this very point. When I did cut my arm this time, and not the wrists, it never bled and simply came back together. Unnerving but kinda cool at the same time. Well, I am dropping my health insurance coverage now as no point in wasting money.

I remembered how *he* travelled and even took me on occasion to travel in that special mode. I willed myself to fly and it didn't work. I did raise about 2 inches of the ground. Although it might be a cool magic trick obviously, the true secret of flight is time, a long time of being immortal. *He* did say *he* was immortal for a long time. Maybe it works like that, you know, the longer you are immortal the better and more enhanced your powers are. It's just a theory and right now I got all the time in the world. Until such time, I am constrained to walking, driving or being chauffeured, or flying First Class. I am not complaining about my current options, would you?

I do not know of any special talents or gifts. Should they have appeared by now? Will I receive an upgrade after I have been immortal for a period of time? So many questions and no answers. The only thing I have to go on is what *he* told me and what talents *he* used. *His* greatest talent was the voice but it clearly is not working for me as I don't hear jack all. I wonder if talents are different to each Immortal? Will I find another Immortal besides Fiona and Sid? Should I just wait until they, those two or others, come to me?

I decided I had enough of Albuquerque and packed up, contacted the caretaker and headed back home to Las Vegas. We shall see what hidden talents are revealed in Sin City. Also, I have to recheck the house to see if *he* might have, just might, left something behind for me. You never know.

I searched high and low in that house and never found one clue or item that I thought was a hint for me that *he* might have left behind for me. Too bad, maybe *he* never realized that I was to become one of them. Or *he* didn't have the talent of sight or seeing the future. Come to think of it, should I go see a fortune-teller or medium to see if they are immortal with the talent? Naw, it can't be that easy, can it?

I tried different things to see what talents may reveal themselves. I practice the levitating and now can get about 4-5 inches of the ground. Hey, it's progress! I spend a lot of time walking up and down The Strip to see what comes about with so many people out and about. I figure the voice or sight or reading people's minds but nothing. It is like I am immortal and that's it. No special power to make the dice roll a certain way or the slots to pay out. What is the fun in this, I am starting to wonder?

I decided to do research and read up and watch everything I can. After countless weeks spent watching movies on vampires, werewolves, Greek Gods and the list goes on and on, I remember one particular movie. It was a Percy Jackson movie and it showed the Greek Gods on Olympus on top of a tall building. That made me think of something and I opted to go visit the tallest building here and I decided to go to the Stratosphere tomorrow. Maybe that's where the current Olympus is located just like in the movie. It has to be better than watching movies all day. It will probably be good for me to get out of the dark house or I will start to shy away from the bright light … literally.

I went up the Stratosphere the very next day. I did wear sunglasses because it was a bright sunny day, not because I was turning in a vampire. At least I hope I wasn't. I get up to the top and walk about enjoying the view from the highest point on The Strip. I do like everyone else does first. I did go look for the hotel, or in my case, go look for where my house is located. After that, I walk around doing a complete circle. I guess the last thing to do is a quick visit to the gift shop. But, I want to get something to drink and sit up here for a bit of time. Thinking, hoping and a moment of wishing for some sort of epiphany.

I grabbed the water bottle and sat down on a bench. It was on the shaded side so I took off my sunglasses to wipe my brow as it getting up there in temperature quickly in the day. I consumed a big gulp of water, it still tastes refreshing, and stare out to the mountains in the distance. A few people walked passed me and I saw colors taking shape around them. Ok, that is weird. I look at some other people to my right and the same thing. It was like a halo of colors but all different shades of reds, greens, blue and such. Now way over to my left, there was one gentleman who had a halo of color, grey, but the intensity of his halo was five grades brighter than anyone else's. He returned the gaze for a second as he noticed I was looking at him carefully and then he disappeared. I thought I was hallucinating or once again, someone slipped a mickey in my drink. But it was none of that as I think I was on to something, a new discovery of a talent. It's possible.

I returned to the gift store where I bought the water, though this time I could see different colors in a halo around every person's head. I grabbed a postcard and a magnet and went to the register to make the purchase. I asked the clerk something innocent like how she was doing.

She replied in a monotonous, "Fine." But then something happened.

Her halo color changed to more a red shade than its original greenish shade. I decided to push her, testing a theory.

"Ae you sure, you don't look fine, dear?"

The clerk snapped back, "YES, I am fine. Everything is fine. Here's your change. Have a nice day." And slams the till drawer closed.

My theory proved correct. The clerks halo changed to a deeper red the more she was lying to me or not speaking the truth to what she was saying. I think I have may discovered my talent: Truth and Lie detection.

OK ok. Not what I was expecting but at least this is fun to play around with. I spend the next few weeks testing it out on everyone and anyone. I developed a chart to the degree a person is honest as they can be or a pathological liar. I love to watch the change in colors when confronted or asked a question by yours truly. I have even called a few people out on it and, of course, where is the first place I head to get some real-world practice? Why, the poker tables at any casino. Oh, I had so much fun there and made a lot of money. Not that I needed it but it is fun to win a little. Why yes, yes, it is!

Oh, this is interesting. I was playing this table at the New York, New York casino and winning a lot but losing every fifth hand to keep the other players in the game. After I just bankrupted one player on a silly bluff and called him out on it, he left the table broke but a new player stepped in. I scanned him but his halo had no normal color, it was pure grey. Hmm, this is the second time I had seen this. I wonder what it means? Does he have a blocker somewhere on his body? Oh, wait a minute, I now realize what he is. I bet you that he is like me.

I stand up. "Alright, I have taken enough of you all's money for today." They all sigh in relief. I turn to the new player "It's your lucky day, would you care to join me for drink? I'm buying!" He springs out of seat, says good-bye fellas and joins me in the lounge where they do the dueling pianos at night.

"You certainly are a unique woman," he replies. His halo turned a lighter shade grey. Interesting.

"Well, sincere flattery may get you more." I bait him to proving more to my lie detection. It seems Immortals' halos are grey by nature. However, the closer to goodness and truth, the lighter or white they become. Whereas, the more evil they are and lying to me, the darker it fades to black. I never tell him what I am though he probably suspects it. We chatted for a bit and I finally pay for his drink and wish him well as he departs. I feel like I am thinking about him. I get this random thought inside my head telling me thanks for the drink and then he is out of sight. Damn, I should have questioned him some more. I vow to question more intensely the next Immortal person I find.

Oh, I did forget to mention I can turn this talent on and off, didn't I? Otherwise, I would have gotten sick from the kaleidoscope of colors 24-7 changing shades every few seconds. I assume *he* did the same thing with the voices.

Armed with the discovery of my awesome talent, I go out into the world with a more positive perspective. I now know how I can use my talent to avenge *his* death. I now have the killers identified, Fiona and Sid. I do have to come out with a way to defeat them as it won't be easy. Revenge killing, I suppose, is never easy. However, I have to seek out others and compile a strategy for taking them both down. There always is a way. Everyone has a weakness, a mortality weakness, for sure they can be destroyed, can't they? If not, then I will die trying to find out.

Ah ha, after months of searching for them I think I have tracked them down. Ok, I found them. Here they come. It is time for some revenge, my way. It is rather amazing to think what has happened to get me to this point.

FATE OF BLACK

This is finally it.

Yeah, Yeah. You all were probably expecting me to talk about how old I am and how I will redeem myself for the greater good. Thus I can live a happy life with a clean, moral conscience. Sorry, this is not that story but I am sure you can find one like that in your local library. Not that you or anyone visits the local library anymore.

No, this is simply a narration of facts. I am what I am and was created to do one purpose. What is this glorious purpose, you are wondering? Simply, it is to propagate the Immortals, both creating them and decommissioning them. Yes, it is a fancy way to say that I kill the Immortals or, in layman's terms, butcher my own children. Sounds kinda funny doesn't it, because Immortals aren't supposed to die. That is true but take my word for it, they are immortal until I take away their immortality. Hey, if I can give it, I can take it away.

Unless of course, they do something stupid in the first 30 days, then they didn't really deserve to be immortal. I did not setup the 30-day rule but it kinda makes sense. Everything else is left up to chance. Pure and simple. Now I may have some fun in manipulating the system, but in the end the system corrects itself, with or without my doing.

Everyone assumes the big man upstairs does not involve himself with trivial matters about the lowly humans down here on good ole planet Earth. Well, if that was the case, then what exactly is our – our meaning us Immortals – purpose then? Did we ever actually need to have a purpose? I mean come on, what is a wasp's purpose other than to annoy humans? Now wait, I am not saying that us Immortals are here to annoy humans, though we do have some fun from time to time. Maybe there is no purpose and we simply exist like the giraffe or the cat or any other species on this planet. We are not the designers rather only the players. We just play by a different set of rules. Too bad for anyone that is not an Immortal as I like to think we have way more fun.

Ok Ok. You want to know more about me. Well, I am 5'8'' and naturally brunette though it changes as much as the clothing styles and hairstyles change from decade to the next decade. Yup. My favorite time-period style was in the 1960's and my least favorite was sometime in the 1400's.

Oh, you probably weren't thinking about *those* details about me. Alright, what exactly do you want to know? How old I am? You can ask me though a proper lady never reveals her true age. Besides, I am older than you think. Way older than even your great great-grandmother and beyond. I think I have met her, kind lady if I remember correctly. In fact, if I told you my age at this very moment, you would go home, turn out the lights, and drink all night in the dark shivering in terror. Yep, we will leave it on the table that I am really old. Enough on this question, move on to the next one.

You are asking if I am so old, then I must have gone by different names over the millenniums? To answer this, yes, you are correct. We have a winner. I could not keep the same name as that would be boring and people would start to catch on eventually. *Hey lady, why haven't you died yet. You should be dead by now. Are you a witch or something?* So, in keeping up appearances and for safety sake, I had to change my name and hairstyle every 50-75 years before I begin to move on. Oh, the things I do to stay within society and keep up with the times. It also means I have to find a corrupt lawyer every so often, easier than you think, to 'will' my wealth and possessions to my next name and identity. In fact, I am so good at this, at some point in my life I attended law school and earned a degree so I could do it myself. Hey, it makes it so much easier now especially with what lawyer's fees are these days.

Getting back to the various names. Yes, I haven't forgotten about your question. People are always paranoid over anything that is not of the norm. It is a common fact. They are even more paranoid especially when a person is different than the group. The proverbial "black sheep" in the flock. But hand it to the common folk, they are witty and creative when it comes to creating exciting names to call me. During the Dark Ages, I was called the **Angel of Death**. The most used name I have heard is the tried and true classic **The Devil.** Excuse me, I am not evil. Well, not entirely but I certainly do not have horns or a tail. And I hate red overall. Then there is my favorite, **The Queen Bee.** Which at first the name stung, but then I got used to it and even started to wear black and yellow for a period of time. And finally, during the Christian movement, I was named the **Fallen Angel** to which I often point out I have no wings and no tattoo of them on my back. Also, if you heard me during NFL football season, there is no angelic voice in me rather a lot of swearing at the TV. Ok, maybe the fallen angel mantra fits after all. You would be swearing like that if you were on shore leave too and if your favorite football team was the……. Nope, not gonna tell you. But you can probably surmise who it is and there is always draft time to build up hopes for next season…. oh nevermind.

There is so much to tell about me I don't know where to begin. Well, I love romantic comedies, long walks on the beach, and red wine. Wait a minute, this is not a dating site. Though I do love red wine and that is a fact. Still I am an older woman, could you handle dating an older woman? I didn't think so. You are welcome to try your best pick-up line but, and you have to trust me on this, I have heard 'em all. The pick-up lines in the 1600's, wow, it makes you wonder if any decent woman would have put out. Then again, who am I am to judge? I am only the creator and destroyer, no judgement bone in here, ironically. Does a mother judge her kids? After all, she "created" them, should she not judge them? Nope, she loves them unconditionally so I follow the same rules. Most of time, at any rate.

Ah ha, you heard me mention the *creating* part, didn't you? Yeah, I figured this would have come up sooner versus later. Everyone wants to know how I do it, why I do it, and what exactly I do?

So, if I came to your workplace and asked those same three questions, could you answer me with much gusto and fanfare? Thought so. Now compare it to me and you realize it is exactly the same thing. Go figure. Yes, but you want to know more and hear the juicy details. Well, here you go.

One of my talents is to create Immortals. The word "gift" is so passé and freak of nature. It is not very flattering. I thought of a better word and came up with "talent", which is more appropriate. If you think you got a better name, then email it to the committee. Yes, I create Immortals from normal, everyday humans and no, I do not "birth" them. That's disgusting to even think of or visualize. Yuck. Anyways, there had to be one who propagates our kind and I am proud to say I am the only one who does the dirty deed. The only one as far as I can tell. Yes, I should have a 5-star rating on any webpage given I am so good. There has been many of our kind and I give it a really good mix-up: shape-shifters, clairvoyance, witches, soothsayers, prophets, mediums, conspiracy-theorists, sports personalities, rich computer geniuses, and the list goes on and on.

Do I have control on what I create? Yes and no. You know, this is never an exact science but I still get blamed for it nonetheless. I can think about what I want to create and maybe I have a 20% chance, tops, of what may come out to be what I wanted or wished for in my mind. Then again, find me better odds in life. I really do awesome work and it is incredible work. Look about yourself if you don't believe me. There are many Immortals that can vouch for me. And the Big Guy upstairs doesn't complain one iota.

On occasion and out of pure randomness, I do "birth" some rather powerful Immortals and once I figure they are more powerful than even me, I try to vanquish them as fast as I can. That, my friend, is not always the case. It used to take me a long time to take them out. I could give you some incidents throughout history but you can go read a history book and wonder why world wars or mass slaughters were started. Yep, sometimes it takes years to hunt them down but I have gotten better at it in the modern era, finally. They still take their toll on humanity as some have decided to follow the path to ultimately attempt at controlling the world. I have taken them all down, one after another or I would not be here telling you this. After all, I have over...... oops, I almost told you how many years old I am. Nice try!

Yes, what I create I also destroy or terminate. No, I am not the terminator! It is a fact of life and certainly in this field of work, it happens all the time. Though I prefer the creating part, I still do the destroying part on equal par. Hence, it makes sense that one of my talents includes shapeshifting. Obviously, I have to sneak up on an Immortal and thus catch him or her off guard so I can terminate their immortality. It's a nifty trick. Flick of the wrists, so to speak. I do try to spice up the song and dance but it is really as easy to take away the immortality as it was to grant it to them. Hey, I don't make the rules, rather I only enforce them. I do try to make it quick before some idiot with a phone starts filming me in the act. Damn technology in this day and age.

Getting back to shapeshifting, it is really, really cool to do. At first I thought, why would I want to change into a wolf or a dog or any other nasty animal for that matter? They smell so awful and I would have to hunt down some other animal if I get hungry and eat the flesh raw. Hey, I do dig a medium rare steak at a fancy restaurant but that's my limit. No raw flesh of a dead animal for me except for sushi, I suppose. I'd rather shift back and walk buck naked into a diner to get my meal cooked.

On second thought, maybe that is not such a good idea. Only then did I finally do it and my first animal to shift into was a grey wolf only because they are so adorable. I then realized a grey wolf did look out of place in the high country of central...what is now called Egypt. Maybe a ram or billy goat might have been a better choice. Still, my wolf fur was quite soft and I did actually enjoy running around.

Note, it took me years and years before I finally even thought about doing it. Only then did I finally shape-shift, only to realize to my amazement, I really do love it. Now, I do it all the time and shape-shift into mostly smaller animals but sometimes into even other humans just because I can now. That talent took a lot longer to master than you would think. You wouldn't have wanted to be around for those first "attempts" – think more of Big Foot type of humanoid. Hmm, now that I think about it maybe someone did take my photo. It really was me, after all this time, and not some freak of nature. Big Foot does not exist nor does Loch Ness. But ghosts, lost cities, UFO's, and whatever is on the list, that's for another discussion.

I digress. It is so much fun to do but sometimes I get lost in who I am unless of course I change into an animal. My favorite animal currently to shapeshift into is, naturally, a wolf. I don't know why but it seems my preference to change into this animal. Eagles are cool too when I want to float along in the sky on a nice summer day. Who wants to change into a bug, by the way? Check me out on Instagram at @WolfLivesDoMatter.

I talked about creating, now is the time to talk about the opposite too. And that is the destroying. Though, after all these ages, I prefer to name it by a better name and I have only come up with "recycling." See, doesn't that sound a lot more pleasant? Are you ready to hear the explanation of the process in killing off the Immortals that I have created? I thought I had peaked your interest and now you get to hear all about it but first we need to take a break for a little backstory.

Think of a time of way back when. Ok. You got a time period pictured in your head? Good. Now go back 400 years. That's where I will start my tale of grandeur and excess. To make it even easier, let's start in the late 1600's where I was a prosperous and well-to-do female living in a time when women were not highly regarded. Still, I kept my cool knowing the women's worldwide liberation movement would eventually get going in another 200+ years. After all, I got all the time in the world to wait. And wait I did.

I managed to find enough "male" companions to persuade with a more liberal understanding to my cause and unique ways. In other words, I did a little convincing by a display of my true powers to help get them aligned to aid me through those dark times. Still, I lived the high life and enjoyed the comforts of the modern-day applications i.e. servants to carry out every task of my daily life. Imagine what some people's life consisted of to take care of my daily needs. I raise a glass to salute all of you all as I was rather high maintenance. I still am today, in case you were asking.

It was in the mid-1700's that I was getting bored with old European ways and wanted some adventure and excitement. I sold the farm and estate, packed up my things (well, had the servants do it) and sailed for the New World. It sounded cool and different and probably a lot of Lords and Barons were much happier to see me gone, hopefully for good.

Once in the New World, I quickly established myself in the Virginia colony as the most prominent bitch on the block. I think this was the time where the "Queen Bee" name might have originated. I don't know. I always saw myself as fair and just. Maybe the servants might have had a different opinion of me – *awful taskmaster, mean-spirited woman, she is so evil, what a bitch, etc.* – but they never said it to my face. Lucky for them, they just gained a few more years of living in service to me.

I brought them all together one day to find out what my people thought of me. I asked them to be frank and honest in their opinion of me. A few people were brave enough to speak out and gave me honest feedback. Pity them. I rewarded their honesty by personally cutting their heads off with a shiny axe. As many know, the axe does not cleanly sever the head from the body immediately. It takes a few swings to truly decapitate the head from the body. It was a good thing I had a decent blacksmith who sharpen the axes so fine, so it only took me two or three swings to complete the task. The blacksmith's name was Sid so you might want to remember this useful tidbit.

I remembered Sid the Blacksmith was a humble man and lived a simple life prior to my appearance in the village. He was never one for strangers or anyone for that matter and preferred to live his life out doing what he loved. That was about to change because I not only wanted him for a specific role I also needed his master blacksmith skills in making weaponry. This was the kind of man I needed, at the time, to assist me in killing the very people trying to kill me.

It did not take long to "convince" Sid of his special purpose in this life and beyond. I guess in the end, he was getting bored with the humble life and now prefers the action and adventure of our current lifestyle. He no longer talks of the olden days, thank goodness, but I think he does miss it everyone once in a while.

Sid and I became the rising stars of the roaring mid-1700's. We became the duo to be reckon with myself being the more out-spoken of the two. There were not many immortal creatures populating the world during this time period. I was no longer in need of Sid's blacksmiths skills yet but there was always a chance someone may decide to take a potshot at me nevertheless.

I thought this was a good time to take a break from it all and actually live a normal life. Though I soon realized there was more to this "New World" and I was never going to have the break I so long sought after. But one does not want to hear boring or sad stories so I will skip toward the more interesting parts. After all, in the hundreds of years that have passed, do you need to know every small detail, every killing and every strange creature I have created, proud or not, and what I have unleased onto the world?

Sid and I eventually jumped on the bandwagon, so to speak, and headed out West for more adventure and excitement. Granted, in those days heading out West meant traveling to what is now the State of Kentucky. Hey, it was thrilling back then. We moved to the area where horses and bourbon would soon rule the land. Though these industries were in their infancy or not even started, they soon would become king of this State. Luckily, we caught it at the right time and our smart investing skills were timed right as we acquired a good parcel of rugged land in what hundreds of years later would become horse country. Little did we realize what it would be worth in present day as we were only thinking of an awesome hideaway out in the sticks at the time. Though I must confess back then, the so-called bourbon that was produced around us years later was a little rougher around the edges, I am glad it got better and tastier over the years.

We 'settled' here in the rough lands for good many years. Sid got a contract to make some of the copper stills that were to be used in many of the bourbon production distilleries and he received the end product, bourbon, as payment in kind. Who can complain about that sort of deal? I started raising horses, ironically, in the beginning as to keep me from getting truly bored. As it turned out, it provided the necessary income for many, many years to come. There were no cars or vehicles back then, if you wanted to get somewhere you walked or rode a horse. I guess it was better than to steal from the banks and other 'sources' of revenue that didn't report it to the police or eventually the government taxman. I much prefer to obtain funds legally but in the end, money is money and accumulation of wealth is what helped keep us going through the millenniums.

Decades went by as we lived as the eccentric rich folks outside of town. Our friends began to die off and people started to grow suspicious of us. Why do we never look unhealthy or never seem to age? We use to tell everyone it was the bourbon and the copious amounts we both drank that was the secret to eternal youth. After a while, the laughs grew quiet as people started to figure out "there was something not quite right with them folks." We started to hear that in a higher frequency and decided to put our holdings with a trusted friend as Sid and I left town and headed out even further West to start all over again.

This time it was to set-up shop in the land that ultimately became the great State of Utah. Sid and I, rather wealthy by then, had a much easier time to transverse the continent when you pay others to do all the dirty work of moving our goods. It was the perks of the lifestyle we were accustomed to, especially after I have been doing this for hundreds of years, even before Sid joined the team. I think we had about 10 extra people, the kind of people that did not ask questions when they were paid much more money than dictated. In fact, many of the workers employed by us were often converted by me at some point. One must always get rewarded for loyalty one employs even when they never realized their true potential in the grand scheme of things.

This was both a blessing and curse. I have and can create some unique and fun immortal creatures, both human and shape-shifting type. So, it was unfortunate the one incident in the mid-1800's. I believe it was shortly after the end of the Civil War when some of my own creations decided it was the perfect time to rebel as well.

I have learned over the years that wars, especially mass-scale wars spanning a continent or many continents, are often a good smoke screen for the immortal creatures to thrive on human bodies. Most common folk would write it off as the atrocities of the war, the dead and mangled bodies found throughout the countryside. Little did they comprehended many of the causalities were not from the enemy but rather my own creatures, more specifically, the pesky werewolves in particular.

After the news of the surrender of the rebels in Virginia at some remote courthouse in the spring of 1865, we thought it would be the beginning of peace, something this country needed after the last four bloody years. However, there was something that happened one does not see in the history textbooks. That was the Werewolf Rebellion of 1865.

At first, the werewolves were a small group keeping to themselves in a few towns in the area of southern Utah. There was no harm as they had plenty of land to roam freely and hunt. Everyone knew their territories and most travelers crossing their hunting grounds would cover it by day, never stopping at night. It was always assumed by folks around here and even the warning of most guides to never be out in those lands alone particularly on a full moon.

Of course, there is always somebody that sparks it all off. In this case, there were two couples making their way to Salt Lake City from Denver. They had to stop in the lands marked 'Do Not Stop' as by luck of the draw one of their horses grew lame. They quickly set-up camp and the men took shifts guarding the camp throughout the whole night, which happened to be a night of a full moon. One can probably figure out what happened next.

First, the young werewolves starting smelling the fresh scent of the humans and immediately began attacking as a pack. The first male guard, Elijah, took out a few of the wolves which angered the pack master even further. He called upon other packs roaming around and eventually three packs rallied together and eliminated Elijah and his wife along with the other couple and the horses too. But all the wolf packs took heavy losses with nine werewolves dead along with a lucky potshot that nailed one of the Pack Masters. This certainly caused a fuss with the survivors of the werewolf packs and enough for the werewolves to break their agreement with the local towns nearby. Over the next three days, many humans and werewolves died senselessly until the elders of the towns and myself came together to broker a truce with the local wolf packs. It was not easy either. The packs accused the humans of breaching the standing agreement and the humans accused the werewolves of not being able to control themselves during a full moon.

I thought of ending this Werewolf Rebellion of 1865 by simply wiping out the entire werewolf population but, in the end, I restrained myself from overextending my true powers. Instead, I took out one overly-talkative pack master who got too lippy, well I should say flashed too many teeth at me and, so, I quieted him down straight away. Soon, the other wolves conceded and the peace treaty was restored with the agreement between the humans and werewolves. I always loved the wolves, it was just sometimes they bite off more than they can chew.

Afterwards, the balance was back to normal and I resumed imbibing in a much longer break from the world and all the crazy shit that accompanies it. I thought it would be the case but I was quite mistaken. You see, world wars tend to bring the various Immortals out from hiding, out from the shadow of darkness and in to the open. When the two world wars dominated most of the first half of the 20th century, I had to deal with all sorts of craziness among my kind. Immortals who thought they could rule the world. Immortals who were decimating small villages that were mistakenly being blamed on the advancing enemy. And Immortals that thought it would be a good time to challenge me, of all people.

Don't get me wrong, I love a good challenge, especially when someone I created and gave power to thinks they could take me down. Well, I am telling you this story so you can only guess who won in the end. This wasn't the first time and certainly won't be the last.

In the 1940's, there came upon an unforeseen dilemma. I had my own, the one's I have created to which I called Pure Bloods. Now these Pure Bloods figured it out as children who ultimately mature as they should do what should not be done. They started creating their own hybrid offspring, aptly called Fake Bloods. I have foreseen it before and see it clearly now: the child or children often rebel against their parent(s) and it would have been a matter of time before the children of the children rebel as well.

Good thing for me, there are rules that govern such occurrences in the universe. One those rules is that if the creator, the Pure Blood, gets killed by yours truly then all of his or hers Fake Bloods die instantly. Now, this was useful to control the population, especially when others were creating these abominations. Yes, it could be called genocide and there was a lot of that going around at the time but I had to correct the balance. Thus, I had to clean my own house and with that, took out a lot of the Immortal rank and file. I felt bad about it but what had to be done must be done. In the end, the Immortals numbers were reduced by over 90% - population control to the extreme or nearly genocide.

Luckily, I had one Immortal who kept *himself* clean and free of the drama and gossip. Add to the fact *he* was not power hungry and simply wanted to exist, it was often best not to intervene with *him*. Later, I found out *he* would be important in the grand scheme of things. Especially since it was *his* protégé, a woman he saved from killing herself, that was hidden from Sid's radar for such a long period of time. It is strange how things come together and for a reason. I start to understand the grand scheme of it all if I really concentrate.

His story was a rather unique one. I thought *he* was rather humble and passive and never gave much thought on how *he* would turn out. *He* was a great man during his time most notably for honor and justice. Thinking back, I could probably have used some decent folks in my ranks and *he* was created at the right time. I was hoping to utilize *his* attitude in my closer circle of trusted, how do I say, advisors, as I felt *he* would never betray my trust.

After *he* was converted to the Immortal ranks, *his* outlook changed dramatically. *He* seems actually pissed off at me and disappeared for many, many years before I came across *his* presence. And that was a chance crossing as well though I assume *he* did not feel me and Sid's presence. I am thinking more *he* choose to simply ignore us. I did not pick up any bad vibration and assumed *he* was leading his own life and doing *his* own thing. I could not complain about that, now could I?

In a bizarre coincidence that was somehow related, Sid was haunted by the most troubling nightmare in a long time. I remember it clearly as though I shared in his pain too. Sid wakes up, sweating and in genuine terror. I calm him with a cup of English tea and once he is steady and breathing returned to normal he shares with me the horrible vision he just experienced.

Sid goes into great detail describing the setting complete with the sights, smells and sounds. I can at best paraphrase his account but be mindful he described it in much more detail.

He tells me we are walking along a forest as the sun starts to set in the evening sky. He can hear the sounds of nature with all the cast of various forest animals and creatures lurking around us. We continue to walk along the path but it is getting darker as the minutes continue to tick forward. We spy a cave up ahead with a torch ablaze at the entrance. How convenient. It starts to rain and the sky grows darker and darker so the cave with the warmth of the lit torch is starting to look more appealing.

We both race toward the cave and he reaches for the torch as we both continue to move deep inside the cave. The sounds of the forest decrease and we no longer hear the rain outside either. We continue to march forward inside this cave, which apparently is larger than we first imagined.

He tells me he hears a strange sound up ahead and we should proceed with caution. We are not armed with any weapons to defend ourselves except maybe the torch but then that is our only light source. We are still walking in this cave and then we come up to a wall ahead of us. We stop in front of the stone wall and see there is a cut in the rock wide enough for one person at a time to move thru. Sid goes first and I am right behind him. The light starts to dim each time he turns a corner in the rock but eventually we make it through and wind up in a large chamber with a large pool of water. We can hear the slow dripping of water droplets splashing in the pool and echoing throughout the vast, dark chamber.

We lean over to look in the pool of water and smile at our own reflections. Is it not what everyone does at a pool of water, right? We both smile at the same time and continue to stare at our own reflections along with the fire from the torch blazing away. I only look for second to the fire in the reflection and back to my own image in the pool. Except, there now a third figure standing next to me in the reflection. Oh My God, I jump back and look to my right but there is no one there!

Sid tells me to calm down and when we look at the pool again, we initially see our own reflections. Except this time, the mysterious figure appears again in the pool and pulls out a sword and swings it toward my head. Sid immediately throws a rock in the water to break up the reflections but I fell back still reaching for my head, to assure myself that it is still attached. Sid tells me that we should get out of here except the cut in the rock is gone. We inspect the rock wall behind us and there is no cut in the rock, no exit other than into the water as there is an opening on the other side of the pool, about 30 feet away.

Sid and I debate about various options and conclude that the exit on the other side of the water pool is the only option. He throws some rocks in the water to test the depth and decides it appears only waist deep and ok to cross. He directs me to go first and will be right behind me.

Now normally I am not a big fan of the water but mind you, this is a vision. Sid's vision at that, so I guess I can do anything including go into a pool of water which otherwise, in the real world, I would avoid.

Continuing on, Sid's vision has us proceeding through the waist deep water. At least, the water was warm and not freezing when he was recanting this to me. I kinda laugh at that point and thanked him for having a safer thought in visions.

Sorry, I am digressing and should get back to telling of the vision.

We step into the water and push forward in the warm and tepid waters of this large pool inside the cave. Remember, we needed to get to the other side, approximately 30 feet away, as our entrance has been sealed but we see the exit on the other side. Ok. We move cautiously thru the water. I am moving quickly in my steps thankfully the ground is solid rock. Sid watches me and our surroundings to ensure our safety. At some point in the crossing, I stumble and go under.

Sid told me I didn't go under for a long period of time but Sid now sees something completely different. He sees a figure, can't tell if male or female, but this figure is moving fast toward them. Sid couldn't even remember if he was still in the water or not. Anyways, he recalls the figure moves quickly toward us, faster than anything he has ever seen move. The figure moves closer to him and splits into two within five feet in front of him. The first split-figure to the left grabs me in the water and strikes me with a kaleidoscope color ball of energy into my chest and I crumble. The second split-figure to the right moves at incredible speed drawing a sword and slashes Sid's throat with a clean slice.

Sid woke up screaming uncontrollably like a man possessed. I have never heard screaming to such an intensity. It was ear piercing and scared the bejesus out of me for days afterwards. He complained of a pain in his neck for days. I still ponder the imagery of this vision for many years and then finally let it fade in the back recesses of my mind until recently.

Sid and I ultimately loved living out West. We absolutely fell in love with all things desert, mesas, dry heat and altitude. So, we have our lovely home and base of operations in Albuquerque. It is a reasonable distance to most things in the USA and without having to deal with the hustle and bustle of the fast-paced Eastern seaboard. Plus, the food is quite unique and oh so delicious.

We decided to take a break from the work stuff and just enjoy life and all the offerings it brings to us. We thought about it and just decided to run away to Las Vegas for a week. Why not? A short break will do us good. Just to break free and live the dream of anything can happen in the land of no regrets. Besides, I felt like I have made enough new Immortals and decommissioned enough for the year that I could use a long-deserved vacation. I met my quota, now it is time to use some accrued leave, so to speak.

One of the benefits of being the queen Immortal is the really cool talents generated. Oh yes, I have the luxury of bestowing some crazy talents to random people throughout the ages. It has been fun, as fun as work can be, but the true test is what talents the recipient gets and how long it takes to manifest. I have seen some take years before they realize what the true talent is and other figure it out or it turns on for them almost immediately. Mind you, I have absolutely no control on this aspect. I wish I could because I fear one day I will create an Immortal that is more powerful than myself or Sid, or combined. Then what happens?

Just to recap. I have some rather powerful talents. Remember, I love using the word talent though gift, skill, luck of the draw all work just as well. These talents are the unique aspects each Immortal is given. And yes, it is totally random as stated earlier. Some can change shapes into various animals or birds. Some hear voices of humans, thoughts or suffering, all the time. Some can detect the truth and honesty with various mechanisms. I assume an Immortal with this talent probably went into the law field and became a judge. Maybe a poker player too. I am only guessing.

I've heard of various modes of transportation is another talent. Be it flying, invisibility, spontaneous jumping, teleportation or re-materializing, whatever. The list is as endless as there are possibilities.

There were some weird talents reported to me on occasion. They actually sought me out and genuinely complained about getting shafted on their mediocre "talent." What was I supposed to do? Hit them again in hopes of them getting something better? It doesn't work like that, my friend. Now take your ability to grow feathers and fly away. Case closed.

You will never hear me complain. I got shape-shifter to the highest degree. The ability to shift into anyone or anything. But wait, there's more. I got the ability to create and destroy Immortals. Yes, it always sounds ironic, doesn't it? The ability to destroy or terminate an Immortal. Kind of goes against the very definition of the word, doesn't it? Well, somebody's got to do the job and I have been doing it for ………oh, I almost said how old I really am. Whoops. You almost got me. Nice try but I ain't telling.

Let's change topics, ok? With the recycling of Immortals, as I like to call it, I have the secondary skill to block and erase Immortals memories. In that way, they won't come hunting me down to kill me. Now, sadly, this talent is not 100% more like in the mid 70% as there has been a few that manage to remember me and find me. Well, there is nothing perfect in the universe.

Sid's talents are also pretty rad. He can shape shift into a werewolf. Yeah, yeah, I know it sounds so passé but it is useful and sometimes fun for him to run around in the moonlight. With the werewolf talent, his sense of smell is impeccable. Yes, this is a special talent because he can smell an Immortal from a great distance and does not have to be in werewolf form to do it, though the range is much greater when he is in wolf form. More importantly, and one of the most bizarre, is his talent to see the future through visions. Yes, you would have assumed he would have opened up a soothsayer shop and made a ton of money running a fortune-telling business. Naw, his visions are random and laced with a lot of symbolism and hidden meanings. The visions can be entertaining sometimes they are not necessarily something to laugh at.

Oh yes, getting back to the story. We decided to take a break and fly off to Las Vegas. The operative word is fly and I can fly like the birds and be invisible too otherwise there would be a lot of concerned phone calls flooding the 911 system. We land smack in the middle of The Strip on a Saturday night and take it all in. Except Sid's radar, or his sense of smell pings a few Immortals in our vicinity. Now, I normally would not be surprised by this revelation except that Sid informs me it is *him.*

Now this does concern me.

Remember, way back when he was created, transformed, given the Immortal gold card, or whatever you want to call it, I shrugged my shoulders and racked it up as another Immortal created. I faintly remember *him* but did not get any bad vibes emanating so I figured *he* was no threat to me. Also, I felt *him* honest and trustworthy so I chucked *him* off the danger list. Well, something has changed. Drastically too and in such a short amount of time. Note: time is not a big concern so when I say short amount of time I could mean a year to 50 years. It doesn't really matter to me so much.

Sid informs me he is getting a bad vibe about this particular Immortal and I swear I feel the same thing. Not bad as in evil but something unusual, what we interpret as more of a threat to us. Someone who definitely could alter the course of the normal path. Someone who could destroy the entire system. Someone that needs to be stopped right away. I suddenly have become more interested in *him* and everyone that is around *him*. In this case, there are two females attached to him. Strangely, one of the females reminds Sid of his horrible vision. Now that's a weird coincidence, and we have to act immediately.

I come to find out Sid has experienced a multitude of visions with this particular man in all of them. Ok then, I declare, I must terminate *his* Immortality. I'd rather not though because I felt *he* was one of the good ones but business is business and the threat *he* poses must be eliminated soon before *he* attempts to take me or the entire system down. It is only a guess but a precautionary one. Better to be safe than sorry.

We wait it out and discover a prime opportunity to strike *him* at his weakest time. *He* was having a tough time with the death of the female colleague *he* had grown quite close to and then followed up with a fight with *his* girl, the protégé. Tonya was her name, I believe, the one *he* apparently saved from her killing herself. Interesting as the puzzle is becoming clearer and clearer.

We track *him* for weeks and finally find the perfect break when *he* is taking a vacation in New Orleans. I begin to bait *him* as we catch him in the Quarter enjoying Cajun cuisine during the day. At least *his* last meal was a rather decent one. Sid and I trap *him* by the Mississippi river and perform the necessary deed. It wasn't the smoothest termination I can certainly declare. We have really botched some pretty bad. Still, we thought we did a decent job until we later realized we were being filmed and it was splashed all over the media in the coming days. Whoops. Technology these days.

The media part we can handle. It was the vengeful girlfriend that was of some concern to Sid and myself. Sid's reply was simply make her one of us. I thought it was a rather risky move but I could see the logic behind it all. We assumed if she understood our kind and saw the bigger picture, she would be less of a threat to me. That was the plan. We trapped her in a park one night and then invited her to our house in the New Mexican desert and converted her with little resistance or trouble. Or so we thought.

It turns out Tonya was the truly gifted one. She inherited a special talent that was quite powerful. Almost powerful enough to compete against even me or Sid. She must have been the hidden threat all along, the antagonist in the vision that has been plaguing us for many, many years. This threat has now been made known to us and now we have to strategize a plan to squelch it. It isn't the first time and certainly won't be the last. However, it's the present danger and we have to plan to thwart it now. What a waste, as I did like *him* but I truly never cared for her.

The roles have reversed as Sid and myself are the now the hunted. Tonya has been developing her skills and trying to recruit others to take us down. It is too bad that such incredible and rare talent as hers is about to be terminated. Does she really think she has a chance to revenge the death of *him*? This is not one of those "love will triumph" stories because her love for *him* is so strong. Nope not even close. She will make a futile attempt to take us out. She has a better chance of taking us out to dinner versus taking us out permanently.

Why do I sound so confident, you say? Oh, there is a reason. I guess I can share it with you. Only, you must promise you will not tell another soul. You see, I really can't die. Well, I can't die again. I died a long time ago and now I have been given an extension. Add to the fact I am not quite human. Well, human as Tonya and *him*. I give her credit for thinking of what cannot possibly be accomplished. Yet, she will try and she will fail. At least she did get the engagement ring even if it was after the fact. Pity on that. It was such a beautiful ring. She would have been so lucky to be with *him*.

I almost forgot. I spoke with *him* the other day. Yes, he is in a happy place and I shared with *him* he will most likely be seeing Tonya real soon. Like within a week or so. *He* smiled though it was a forced smile. He did pass along a message so I can say something to Tonya in her attempt to hunt us down. Maybe it was a benign plea to spare her life so she lives for a longer time. Hmmm, I kind of have animosity against people who try to kill me even if they don't realize they cannot fully do it.

Speaking of which, I too have something to pass along that I almost forgot. One of the other names I used to go by is Mother Nature. I guess that would have been important to know from the beginning but sometimes it is just for the enjoyment of it all. As if on cue, here comes Tonya. I should decide now to let her live or let her be reunited with *him* very soon. I will let the color of her soul make the decision for me though it has already been decided.

One should never challenge Mother Nature. I always win.

R.J. Matthews began writing down his creative thoughts in 2015. Born and raised in Michigan, R.J. enlisted in the Army and became an intelligence analyst over his 10-year military career. He saw time in Hawaii, Texas, Bosnia-Herzegovina, and England. After leaving the Army he moved to Harrogate, England and joined the British Police staff. Returning to the United States in 2011, R.J. settled in Asheville, NC, met his beautiful wife, and started working for the Department of Veterans Affairs. He and his wife are on a quest to visit all 31 NHL arenas.

www.ingramcontent.com/pod-product-compliance
Lightning Source LLC
Chambersburg PA
CBHW070753120626
46557CB00002B/578